the Christmas Lamp

Also by Lori Copeland

LORI COPELAND

the Christmas Lamp

a novella

ZONDERVAN®

ZONDERVAN.com/
AUTHORTRACKER
follow your favorite authors

ZONDERVAN

The Christmas Lamp
Copyright © 2009 by Copeland, Inc.

This title is also available as a Zondervan ebook.
Visit www.zondervan.com/ebooks.

This title is also available in a Zondervan audio edition.
Visit www.zondervan.fm.

Requests for information should be addressed to:

Zondervan, *Grand Rapids, Michigan 49530*

Library of Congress Cataloging-in-Publication Data

Copeland, Lori.
        The Christmas lamp : a novella / Lori Copeland.
            p.   cm.
        ISBN 978-0-310-27227-4
        1. Christmas stories. 2. City and town life — Missouri — Fiction. 3.
    Missouri — Fiction. I. Title.
    PS3553.O6336C48 2009
    813'.54 — dc22   2009018431

Interior design by Christine Orejuela-Winkelman

Printed in the United States of America

09 10 11 12 13 14 15 • 20 19 18 17 16 15 14 13 12 11 10 9 8 7 6 5 4 3 2 1

To my family: Lance, Randy, Maureen, James, Abi, Anabelle, Joe, Josh, Rick, Shelley, Audrey, Russ, Gage, and Grandma Opal. Love you forever.

Special thanks to Sue Brower, a woman who has allowed me to write my passion in Christmas stories.

Roni walked to the break room refrigerator and took out a piece of cheese and a handful of grapes. Bumping the door closed with her hip, she heard it; the telltale sound of a crash, and then lights and ornaments hitting the pavement.

Judy sprang from her chair. "Good grief! This is a record even for Nativity."

Moving to the window, the women peered out. Roni heaved a sigh of disbelief when she spotted a silver Acura SUV buried in spruce. Tinsel dangled from the headlights.

A man peered out the driver's side window. Moments later the tall, well-dressed man wearing corduroy slacks and a sports shirt unwound his frame from the driver's seat and got out of the vehicle.

Closing her eyes, Roni drew a deep breath and announced. "The new consultant is here."

The two women reached the door simultaneously. Bounding toward the accident, Roni quickly assessed the situation. The city crew seemed untouched. One or two looked slightly dazed, but the consultant's expression was more "what hit me" than angry. "Is everybody okay?" Roni called as she approached the chaotic scene.

"I'm fine," the newcomer said. He glanced at the workers. "Anyone hurt?"

The men shook their heads, eyes scanning the mess. Roni extended a hand. "You must be the new consultant."

He took the outstretched hand. "Jake Brisco."

"Roni Elliot. I manage the City Administration Office." Her gaze assessed the dark-haired consultant, and then moved to the third finger of his right hand. Empty. Her eyes snapped back. "I am so sorry. Someone should have warned you about the tree."

Jake brushed spruce needles off his slacks. "Does it always sit in the middle of the intersection?"

"Always," Roni assured with a smile.

And it always got hit. Nativity wouldn't be itself without their holiday decorations. And the tree was always first to go up, and the first to come down. Literally. It was hit at least twice every Christmas, and sometimes more.

"Well." Jake studied his vehicle, hands on his trim hips. "I guess there's no real harm done."

"Come inside while they clean the mess off," Roni invited. "We have fresh coffee."

"No thanks." He set to work picking tinsel out of the bumper. "I'm going to check into my hotel room. I'll be in first thing tomorrow morning."

Roni glanced at Judy, who was busy assessing the new boss. She glanced at Roni and gave her a thumbs-up.

Was she kidding? The man couldn't drive! Roni turned back to Brisco, who was now crouched on his hands and knees parting the spruce. "You're Mary Parson's grandson?"

"That would be me." He tossed a handful of boughs aside, grumbling under his breath.

"We heard you were coming." For the past few weeks that had been the town buzz. The new consultant is coming. Mary Parson's hotshot grandson. Everything is going to be different. The town will be saved. She assessed the good-looking Superman. Right. He couldn't miss a twelve-foot spruce sitting in the middle of the intersection.

This man was going to save Nativity from going under?

That evening, Roni locked the office, relieved to have the hectic day behind her. Jake Brisco wasn't exactly friendly, but then having a spruce hit your fancy car, as Mom used to say, "would sour a body's disposition."

The new consultant had appeared to have a sense of humor. Once they separated his car from the tree, he calmly picked spruce needles out of his grill and noted that his decorating was done for the year. Roni was grateful he wasn't coming into work until morning. There'd be a little breathing space between the incident and getting down to business.

"Merry Christmas!"

Roni turned to see Dusty Bitterman, who owned the insurance office two doors away, striding toward her. The affable grandfatherly figure flipped her a piece of peppermint candy.

She caught it with both hands. "Thanks, Dusty. You're my first holiday greeting of the season."

"It's the best time of the year. You doing okay this fine day?"

"Never better."

"I'm on my way to see Mary. I understand her grandson blew through town earlier."

Blew through was correct. Mary Parson lived on the outskirts of Nativity, a woman who rarely joined community activities anymore even though she'd been a founding area resident. Folks said that until she had her first heart attack she'd been involved with everything, but once her husband passed away she'd turned into a recluse. Everyone knew of Mary but most knew little about her. Dusty visited her weekly to see if she needed anything, but even he admitted that she rarely did, and that she preferred her solitude.

Sobering, Dusty bent forward. "You know the plan if this thing gets out of hand."

Ronnie nodded. "Ten-four."

Tipping his hat, he walked on as Roni turned toward home. Dusty worked hard to keep the season. He'd lost a nine-year-old son fourteen years ago about this time of the year, so the holiday held even more significant meaning to him. The boy had chased a baseball into a line of traffic. Though Roni was a distracted teenager at the time, she could still remember the sight of Dusty sitting in the middle of a busy highway, all traffic stopped as they watched the grieving father cradle his son's lifeless form, rocking the child gently back and forth.

After that tragic day, Dusty was determined to keep Pete's legacy alive. The boy loved Christmas and all that went with it.

Turning up the collar of her light jacket, she started toward home. The house was a short walk from the office, so she didn't need to invent an excuse to exercise. Her aging blue Volkswagen convertible remained in the garage until Saturdays, when she did her shopping.

A smile touched the corners of her mouth as she thought of the new consultant's arrival. Residents expected the town tree to be knocked over. It wouldn't be a Nativity Christmas if it sat untouched for the next five weeks, but the incident had to be disconcerting to the newcomer.

Drawing a deep breath of fresh air, she dismissed the worry. The annual tree lighting would take place this Saturday night and then holiday activities would be in full swing.

"Roni! Merry Christmas!"

She spotted a familiar face. "Merry Christmas, Wilma. How's Lowell today?"

"I took him to the doctor this morning. He's doing fine. Just a case of indigestion."

"Good—It's nice to see you." By now Steil's Hardware was coming up. Usually Roni breezed right past the store. Hammers and screwdrivers didn't interest her, though she was handy with both tools. Aaron Steil stood in the window setting up a Christmas display.

And then she saw it. The lamp. A gaudy, black-net stocking leg with a fringed shade, an exact replica of the one featured in the movie *A Christmas Story*.

Her gaze riveted on the object. The sight brought back rich memories of the hours she'd spent watching the classic movie with her mom and dad. Images of Ralphie, the kid who longed for a Red Ryder, carbine-action, two-hundred-shot, Range Model air rifle for Christmas raced through her mind. The renowned line rang in her head. *You can't have a BB gun, kid! You'll shoot your eye out!*

Aaron waved and Roni lifted a finger, pointing to the price tag.

He frowned, and she motioned to the white ticket dangling on the cord. Tracing her gaze, he brightened and glanced at the price then mouthed, one ninety-nine.

A hundred and ninety-nine? Dollars? He had to be kidding. He held the lamp closer to the window, brows lifted expectantly.

She shook her head. No. Too much. She couldn't.

Smiling, he set the lamp on a round table and pulled the chain. Soft light pooled over the sidewalk where Roni stood. The effect brought a lump to her throat. Mom. Christmas! The smell of fresh pine in every room, cookies baking in the oven. When Mom was alive she had insisted on a fresh cut tree every season, and Roni still observed the tradition. It wasn't Christmas until a huge tree filled the parlor corner, decorated with childhood ornaments and family keepsakes.

It was silly to continue family traditions with no one to share them with, but she did — and most likely she always would, but she needed to start her own customs.

She'd turned into a creature of habit. Her biological clock wasn't exactly running out, but her dream of filling the house with children had started to look less likely. She'd be thirty in January, and there was not a marriageable prospect in sight. Nativity had only a few single men, and she didn't get to Springfield or Branson that often.

Life was passing her by, but she had no inclination to stop it. She was content, even happy, with small-town life. She made sure that she was involved with community work, and the town was her family.

Darkness closed in as she continued to stare at the funky lamp until the wind picked up. Dry leaves skipped across the street and landed in yards already piled high with dying vegetation.

Snuggling deeper into her jacket, she took a final look at the lamp, and then walked home to her empty house.

2

"Coffee, Miss Elliot?"

Roni glanced up to find Jake Brisco standing in front of her desk. For a second she fixed on his cobalt blue shirt and marveled at the way the color brought out the darkness of his eyes. The man was drop-dead gorgeous. Startled, she shoved the financial spreadsheet aside. "Yes, right away, Mr. Brisco." Pushing back from the desk, she got up and started for the coffeemaker when he stopped her.

"No. Do *you* want coffee?"

Her? Pausing, she glanced over her shoulder.

He flashed a smile, his eyes sparkling with what seemed to be mischief. "How do you take it? Black? Cream and sugar?"

"Cream."

"Cream it is." He motioned to her desk. "Don't let me disturb you."

Jake Brisco was getting *her* coffee? She drew a deep breath. That was a refreshing change. She eased back to her desk and sat down.

Judy cleared her throat. "Good morning, Mr. Brisco."

"Morning, Judy."

Coffee, and he remembered names. Roni shook her head in disbelief.

He poured the coffee into three foam cups, added cream to two, and turned to Judy. "How do you take your brew?"

The clerk sent Roni a curious glance. "Black?"

By eight thirty, the administrative staff: Roni, Judy, and part-timer Tess Miller, were in their seats in the break room. Mayor Stance came in and joined the group a few minutes late.

"Good morning, ladies."

"Good morning, Mayor," the women parroted.

Stance smiled. "How's the sick young'un this morning, Judy?"

"Kept me up half the night. It's just croup, but the two older ones will probably have it by tomorrow."

"Ah, the joys of parenting." The mayor lifted a bushy brow in Roni's direction. "Coffee?"

"Yes, sir. Right away." She got up and poured the liquid, then added heavy cream and two packets of sugar.

Jake rifled through a stack of papers when she returned to her seat. "I trust we're ready to get down to business?"

Baritone, Roni noted. Clear, oozing authority, but nice enough. She wondered how long the pleasant manner would last.

He looked up and met her eyes. "It seems Nativity has a problem."

"Not much of one," the mayor assured. "We could have solved this on our own, given enough time." He cleared his throat with a watery hack. "But no one listens to me."

Luckily, Mayor Stance's objections had been voted down, but it still wasn't likely he'd take to change easily. Yet he loved this town, so Roni figured he'd do what it took to help the town survive.

Stance continued. "We've hit a little financial rough patch, that's all. Since the new highway bypassed us, we've had trouble keeping businesses. All we need are some fresh ideas on how to do that, and we'll be in fine shape."

Jake glanced at the spreadsheet. "Last night I went over the annual revenue, numbers of employees, and payroll expenditures."

Tess sat up straighter. "I'm not going to be laid off, am I?"

Roni glanced at her. The retired librarian openly confessed that giving up work wasn't what she expected. She couldn't live on her social security and small pension, so she had sought a part-time job. The widow depended on the extra income and was worth every cent the town paid her, as far as Roni was concerned.

Brisco frowned. "I'm not here to disrupt lives, Mrs. Miller; I'm here to find solutions to the town's problems. Looking at the situation from a purely 'cutting corners' aspect, we'll need to start with the small things and see if we can get the town solvent without taking drastic measures."

Roni relaxed. Maybe he wasn't going to be hard-nosed and impractical about this. A nip here, a tuck there, and everything would be fine.

Her gaze drifted out the window and toward the street, where the city crew restored the annual tree. Christmas wasn't the time to cut jobs or put poor widows out of work. Her thoughts skipped to the decorations waiting in her attic. Soon she could start festooning her house with holiday splendor—

"Would you agree, Miss Elliot?"

Roni's gaze snapped back. "I ... would certainly give the matter serious consideration."

What had he said? What was she giving serious consideration?

Jake nodded. "Good. It's a small thing, but the little things are what we're looking for. Moving on, let's discuss the town tree."

Easing forward, Roni poised her pen. Undoubtedly, next year he'd want to make the spruce smaller and less—obtrusive.

Jake's eyes fixed on the report. "How many times a season is the tree knocked over?"

The women exchanged glances.

"Once," Judy said.

"Maybe a couple of times," Roni corrected.

"At least three," the mayor amended. "Admittedly it sits in a bad place, but it looks so good in the intersection, so we've left it."

"Three?" Jake's brow lifted. "And each time you replace the decorations?"

"Not all of them, of course," the mayor said. "But we do go through a bunch of lights and ornaments. I wouldn't expect a newcomer to understand, but it's sort of a town tradition." He leaned back, smiling. "Christmas wouldn't be Christmas without our tree, and Nativity wouldn't be Nativity if the tree didn't get knocked down now and then."

Jake rubbed the back of his neck. "About the decorations. You continue to use the old bulbs instead of the energy efficient ones?"

"Why, yes. The energy efficient bulbs cost more, and besides, there's something special about those old bulbs. You know—"

"Tradition," Jake provided. He turned a page. "Have you considered a nativity scene instead? I saw a large church on the corner of Chadwick and Lucas on the way over. It appears to be on the main track, and well suited for a holiday decoration."

Tess entered the conversation. "That's my church. We have a live nativity scene the Sunday before Christmas. The congregation supports the endeavor through our offerings. I don't think folks would take kindly to anyone other than us doing the scene."

Jake lowered the paper. "There has to be a more appropriate place for the tree other than in the middle of the street. Drivers turn the corner and they're on the thing before they realize it."

Everyone shifted as the atmosphere took on a strained feel. Roni tensed. Now he was messing with the big things.

"Shall we move on?" Judy voiced Roni's thoughts.

Jake paused. "Not so fast. I agree we've spent a lot of time discussing the tree, but sacrifices are needed. I suggest that we start the painful process of getting the town back on budget by doing away with the tree if it's hit again."

Before he could move on, the mayor intervened. "Let's not be hasty, Brisco. One unfortunate tree incident isn't cause for panic."

Yeah. Let's not be hasty, Roni silently mimicked.

The consultant held his ground. "I ran a quick tally on the price of replacing lights, tinsel, and ornaments, and the hourly crew cost of the work. The total will surprise you."

"Oh?" The mayor frowned.

Mentally sighing, Roni thought of all the times she'd put the tree cost on Stance's desk and he'd shoved it aside. It was costly, but well worth the expenditure.

"Each time the tree is knocked down, the restoration price tag is over three hundred dollars. If that happens three times every year, the annual cost is almost a thousand dollars." He glanced at Tess. "That amount equals, say, a month's pay for a part-time employee."

Roni shook her head. "But we've always had a tree . . ."

His tone remained the same. "We're on a quest to cut corners. We need to begin with the tree."

"But the tree is already up for the season," Roni argued. "It would be senseless to take it down now."

"But if the cost to put it back up is someone's job . . ." Tess reminded.

Roni couldn't argue. Tess had the most to lose from these fiscal cuts. She glanced at the usually town-loyal part-timer and knew she was worried about her income.

"The tree's up now," Brisco explained, "and if it stays up we don't have a problem. But next year the town should revisit the idea of decreasing the tree size and setting it in a more suitable place."

"You know, this isn't just about tradition; this is about Christmas — bringing the community together, good will to all men and that stuff," Roni noted.

Jake nodded, thoughtful, and then moved on. "So, can I see by a show of hands that we're in agreement?"

"Regarding?" the mayor asked as though he'd just shown up.

"The annual Christmas tree. If it's hit again it won't be replaced."

Roni's hand shot up. "Wait a minute. We haven't fully discussed this matter. You can't just take away our tree!"

All eyes shifted to the window where the chore of resurrecting the tree continued, the shiny ornaments and glistening tinsel lending a festive air to the grave conversation.

Roni knew the tree would go down again before long. Should she do her civic duty and go along with Jake's suggestion, or follow her heart and vote to keep the tree, regardless of the cost.

Her heart won out. She stuffed her hand under the table, praying that God would send only observant drivers to Nativity during the Christmas season.

Tess and the mayor each timidly lifted a hand.

She'd lost. Resentment burned Roni's cheeks and she refused to look at Brisco. She couldn't imagine the town without a Christmas tree.

He turned to face the window, moving on. "I see you have a nice gazebo. Do you utilize it during the holidays?"

Mayor Stance cleared his throat. "Of course. We've built it extra large so we can install an ice rink for the holiday season."

Jake frowned. "An ice rink? In Nativity?"

Roni had anticipated his concern. Missouri's winter months were fickle; cold one day, and hot the next. The state received its share of bitter wind, snow, and ice, but no one could predict with accuracy when the storms would hit.

Stance nodded. "We rent a portable rink that produces enough ice for a small skating arena. Granted, it is a considerable expense, but the town wouldn't think of giving it up."

"Exactly how much does this artificial ice rink cost?"

"Well, the cost depends on the size, the rental period, and the weather. We can't always count on low temperatures, so the fee includes the cooling units, a buffer tank, and generators. We also pay the insurance and electric expenses. The rental company provides the skates. Volunteers serve as supervisors and security, but we have to rent proper lighting. We've done it for years. It's a real holiday boost to our business district."

Roni's lips firmed. The rink and the concessions boosted Nativity's economy. Wasn't that the idea? To fill the town coffer?

Judy tapped a pencil on her legal pad. "My kids would die without that rink. It wouldn't be Christmas without it."

Jake sobered. "Would you rather give up the ice rink or emergency services for the town?"

A hush fell over the meeting.

Jake moved on. "I understand the town has an annual home decorating contest?"

"Oh yes—we love that." Roni shifted in her chair. "Everyone in town decorates, and we have a committee that judges the entries."

"And there's a three-hundred-dollar prize to the winning house," Tess noted.

Nodding, Jake perused a paper. "It says here there's a parade?"

"Every year," Roni confirmed. "We have it at night, with lighted floats."

"Sounds nice," Jake laid the paper on the desk. "I'm assuming that businesses fund the floats?"

"Oh definitely," Roni replied.

"Well then." Jake looked up. "This gives me a lot to work with. That's all for today; thanks everyone."

3

Roni had to hand it to Brisco. The man was focused. Poring over financial, administrative, and public records, he'd spent the entire day in the office. Behind his back, Judy gathered punch and ordered cookies from the bakery for the surprise welcome party planned for after hours.

"If this town is so darned broke, who's paying for Brisco's services?" Judy asked as she applied fresh lipstick in the lady's room.

Assessing her hair in the mirror, Roni wondered the same thing. Usually she would be consulted about these types of matters, but the mayor hadn't said a word. "I haven't a clue."

"It has to be Dusty Bitterman." Judy worked her lips and then bent to smooth the color evenly. "He's the only one around with that kind of money."

"Could be." Roni ran a brush through her hair. "But Dusty wouldn't let Brisco change anything. Christmas in Nativity is too special."

"You'd bet on that?"

Nodding, Roni dropped the brush into her purse. "If I were a betting woman."

The informal welcoming party took place around five o'clock. Roni noticed that Jake had discretely ignored the hushed conversations around the coffee machine. "All of this in my honor?" Jake asked, following up with a friendly warning. "You may want to retract the gesture before month's end."

"We already regret the gesture," Roni muttered under her breath. She wondered if Tess and the mayor would find Brisco so charming once cutbacks were instituted.

Over bites of sweets, Tess familiarized Jake with the office's daily routine. The mayor didn't stick around long; he just ate a cookie and then begged off with the explanation that he had to attend his grandson's basketball tournament.

While Roni cleaned up, Judy and Tess started to put out the annual office Christmas decorations: holly, Santa faces, a sleigh filled with colorful ornaments. The archaic aluminum tree with blue ornaments needed to be pitched, but Mayor Stance wouldn't hear of it.

"Are Tess and Judy on the clock?" Jake whispered to Roni as he slipped into his leather jacket.

"No." *Great.* By the end of the meeting this morning, it was apparent to all that he *was* going to disturb the usually tranquil waters. While Judy and Tess hung wreaths, Jake counted pennies. Judy still had to fix supper for her hungry family, and Tess mentioned that she needed milk before she went home. They were all tired. And he was complaining. "We don't work on a clock. We operate on an honor system," Roni explained.

"Honor system." Jake zipped up his jacket. "That's a little lax, isn't it?"

"Not for this office. The employees are honest and give a fair day's work." Why did she have a feeling he'd soon have them punching a time clock?

Sometime during the afternoon, clouds had moved into Nativity, and by the time Roni walked out of the office a light freezing drizzle left a glaze on sidewalks and windowpanes. Missourians had a saying: "If you don't like the weather, stick around an hour and it'll change." Roni could testify to Mother Nature's fickle moods.

After locking up, she turned to see Jake scraping ice off his Acura's windshield and she moved to assist. She'd do it for the mayor, so she supposed she could try to mend fences and help, even though she felt anything but charitable toward Brisco. "Got an extra scraper?"

"Yeah, thanks." Jake reached in the running car and located a second implement. Passing the scraper to her, he then proceeded to bust a thin ice coating off the door handle. "This rolled in quick."

"That's Missouri for you." Roni started on the frozen windshield. "You're from Springfield, right?"

"Actually, I was born and raised near Ava, but I moved to Springfield when my parents and sister were killed in a car accident."

Her scraper paused. "I'm sorry."

He glanced over. "It was a long time ago. My dad's sister took me in. We made it fine." He yanked the handle and the sound of cracking ice shattered the cold air. "What about you?"

"Lived in Nativity all my life." She corrected. "Well, not *all* my life yet, but I was born in the upstairs bedroom in Mom's old house." The same patchwork quilt was still on the bed that had been on Grandma's mattress. Roni had left the home undisturbed when Mom died. Everything, including the kitchen linoleum, was the same as it was the day Roni was born.

"Married?" he asked.

"Nope. Engaged once to a nice guy, but then my dad died and my mom got sick. I put my personal life on hold to take care of her." She lifted a wiper blade.

"Yeah?" Moving from the cleared side windows, Jake walked around the car and started on the back glass.

"What about you?" she called.

"Me? Single. Boring."

"I doubt that." A man with his looks wouldn't go unnoticed by the opposite sex. He reminded her of a dark-eyed Patrick Dempsey. Only Dempsey had hazel eyes. She thought. Actually, she didn't know. But Brisco reminded her of him. The way he looked right at her with those smoldering eyes. A quick flash of a dimple in his right cheek.

"Don't doubt it. I'm a workaholic. Ask anyone who knows me."

He had to be near her age—maybe a few years older. It was comforting to know that she wasn't the only holdout around. "No marriageable prospect in sight?"

"There probably would be if I took the time to look, but the truth is I don't look. I've been accused of being too picky, and it's probably an accurate assessment. I've yet to meet a woman that I'd want to share my life with, and one that doesn't go berserk during the holidays."

No wonder he was still single. Roni continued work on the thick layer of ice. Yet she could identify with his pickiness. If the right prospect fell from the sky she'd probably think about marriage, but one hadn't fallen, and at this point in her life she didn't have time to do much other than eat, breathe, and work. "How long have you been with Patton Consultants?"

"Five years. How about you?"

"I started part-time in the city administrator's office when I was a junior in high school."

Pausing, he grinned.

She glanced up. "What?"

"I'm surprised I haven't seen you around."

"From what I hear you didn't visit Nativity that often." Rumor was that he'd rarely visited during his youth, and that only in the past few years had he grown closer to his grandmother.

He nodded. "Touché." Jake pulled his gloves off with his teeth. "The mayor seems like an okay guy."

"He is. He's not much of a leader, but he ran for the office uncontested. Still, he's a nice guy, just not motivated."

The defrosters finally started to clear the ice away. They paused to catch their breath. Leaning against the hood, Roni rested her back. "I don't know if I've said this, but welcome back."

"Thanks. Grandma loves this town."

"It's a town with a lot of money worries." Her gaze shifted to the gazebo. "Until three years ago we were growing. Branson tour buses came through every day from April to January and stopped so folks could go to the Dairy Dream. Now the place can barely keep its doors open." Her gaze traced the large graveled parking lot the owners had built to hold the big buses. Today it sat empty, like the dreams the Dairy Dream had once fostered.

Dot and Frank Henry had worked hard there, trying to eke out a living for their four kids and themselves, but in October Frank admitted he would have to winterize the building or close for the season. Without those buses, local business didn't bring in enough to pay the utility bill. They'd found breast cancer in Dot last summer and she was taking treatments. Frank admitted he had run out of luck.

The light drizzle saturated Roni's light jacket, beginning to sink into the fabric.

Jake glanced around. "Can I help you clean your car?"

"Thanks, but I walk. I only live a few blocks away."

"Then let me give you a lift."

"Thanks again, but I need the exercise." She turned up the collar of her coat. "See you tomorrow?"

"I'll be here. Eight o'clock."

Leaving him standing at his vehicle, she walked off, carefully picking her way across the glazed sidewalk. She'd worn a low heel this morning, never thinking that the weather would turn bad.

When she reached Steil's Hardware she paused to admire the Christmas lamp. Its peaceful warmth lit the gray day. For the first time in years she allowed her mind to consider what her life would have been if she had married Paul. Young and in love, she'd accepted the young county worker's proposal six years ago. Then Mom got sick and Roni had to make the painful decision to commit either to Paul or to a possibly long, drawn-out parental illness. Paul wanted children immediately, and she knew that if she had Mom's full care that kids weren't a possibility. In the end, duty won out. She broke the engagement. Paul was now happily married with two young children, and she was still single and working for a failing administrative office. By now she could have had a comfortable home, two children, security, and a family to go home to every night and share her day.

Her breath formed white vapors as she visualized the leg lamp in Mom's front parlor window—her window now. She had the whole empty house to herself and Mom's cat, Mimsy. It was time that she formed her own traditions. Mom would be horrified by the cheesy lamp, but tastes varied, and it was her life now.

The neighbors would think she'd lost her mind if she stuck that tacky lamp in the window. Yet if she had the money she'd buy the thing in a second. The more she looked at it the more she wanted it.

Aaron's face popped up and he pointed to the lamp, grinning.

Shaking her head, she playfully turned both empty coat pockets inside out and let them hang.

Frowning, he wagged his finger and directed her eyes to the newly erected poster. *Christmas Comes But Once a Year!*

True, but utility and gas bills arrived monthly, and they both wanted their money. They didn't see the holiday in the same carefree manner as others. As much as she wanted the lamp, it would have to wait until another year.

Who knew, if Jake Brisco was all about cutting Christmas traditions now, it might not be long before he was into eliminating jobs. She had seniority, and the town couldn't run without administration, but if times got any worse, Nativity could cease to exist. Jake never cared about the town; he'd never visited his grandma unless forced to.

The lamp looked even more fanciful.

Shaking her finger at Aaron, she moved on. Mimsy would be waiting for her at the back door, expecting dinner.

As she walked home she consoled her loss with the thought that at least something would be waiting for her. She dodged an icy spray from a delivery truck as it flew past. She detested bad weather, and if this stuff stuck around, winter would be early this year.

She had slipped the key into the lock when she sensed it. Then the faint "tinkle" of breaking glass reached her ears. The speeding delivery truck came to her mind.

Stepping back to the edge of the porch, she leaned out to look for the tree, and sure enough, it was gone.

Picking her way out to the sidewalk for a better look, she spotted the truck driver standing in the intersection. The pavement had just enough glaze to be treacherous. He took off his hat and wiped his eyes.

Heartsick, she turned back and made her way onto the porch where she rested her head against the front door panel.

There went the tree.

If she knew Jake Brisco, which admittedly she didn't, when he said something he meant it. She made a mental note to cancel Saturday night's annual tree lighting.

Nativity had just suffered their first fiscal cut.

Jake rifled through a sheaf of papers, his mind on Grandma's frantic phone call this summer. *You have to come save my town, Jake. You're smart like your grandfather. You'll know what to do. I go out so little lately, but I still love my town and its people. I can't sit by and watch it die.*

As soon as he could get away he'd taken a leave of absence, and now here he was. Why, he had yet to figure out. These people were hung up on tradition; they'd gone nuts every holiday and now their town was in trouble. Granted, the new highway hadn't helped, but their holiday expenditures could put even the best of towns into the red. He detested Christmas and all its phony sentiments. Couldn't a man believe in the Almighty without all the gimmicks?

Roni's voice drew him back to his purpose. Clearing his throat, he said, "Believe me, I'd rather be Bob Cratchit standing before you this morning than Ebenezer Scrooge."

His gaze met the grim expressions in the room, and he realized the office staff failed to appreciate the humor.

Judy's face was a combination of fatigue, horror, and confusion. Roni looked like a child who'd had a prized Christmas toy snatched from her hand.

Tess just looked confused.

Jake didn't relish his role as bad guy; these were honest, hardworking small-town folks who valued tradition. But if he was to help Grandma save her town, he had no other choice.

"Not all the tree decorations broke this time."

Jake glanced over. Her mind was still fixated on that tree.

Roni fidgeted with a paperclip. "Actually, it would take very little to replace them."

"This time?" Jake shook his head. "I've been in Nativity for two days and the tree's gone down twice."

Roni's muffled, "You hit it first," surprised everyone, including Jake.

"Pardon?"

"Agreed," she acknowledged. "But the town can't help it if a motorist can't see an object the size of a barn." She met his steady gaze and her thoughts were clear. She'd lived in this town all of her life and *she'd* never hit the tree.

Judy ran a hand through her messy hair, which Jake noted looked as though she'd thrown it up into the air and jumped under it that morning. "Man, Duke and I work our fannies off. We don't eat expensive dinners out. We don't go to the movies or buy our clothes anywhere but Kmart—our biggest treat is taking the kids to Walmart on Friday nights, having a fast-food hamburger, and doing the grocery shopping. Christmas is the only time of year we get to forget that we're poor and just enjoy the season. Christmas won't be the same without the big tree."

"I'm sorry, Judy. I hear you, but we have to start somewhere," Jake focused on Roni. "You'll inform the media of the change?"

She nodded, tight-lipped. It didn't take a clairvoyant to know her heart wasn't in the agreement.

Off to a great start, Jake. Alienate the staff, especially this one. Roni was intelligent and sensible; nobody liked the cuts, but she would see the wisdom in his decision. So why was it so hard to witness the childlike disillusionment in her eyes? She loved her town.

When he was a kid he'd found every excuse to avoid holidays in Nativity, a tiny burg in the middle of nowhere. During his teen years he'd been obnoxious about the holidays, and his conscience still hurt when he thought of all the times he'd argued with his aunt about the subject. He'd didn't want to leave his friends and spend the holiday with Grandma—a woman he barely knew.

Judy blew her nose.

"Okay, moving on to purchasing expenditures." He glanced up. "Does this office really use five boxes of paper clips a month?"

After work, Roni stopped at the bakery for a loaf of Limpa Rye. During the holidays Jolsen's Bakery featured a different type of bread every day. Limpa Rye was a favorite of Roni's elderly neighbor, and she liked it okay.

Stepping into the fragrant establishment, she wasn't surprised to see that this one business was thriving. This time of year brought a tremendous increase in bakery revenue, so much so that Eugenia, the owner, was talking about getting rid of her old gas-guzzler and purchasing one of those subcompact models.

"I'll be right with you!" Eugenia called over the heads of a sea of customers waiting to buy. Some were taking their time about their selections. Roni located an empty table and sat down. The pleasant aromas of cinnamon and nutmeg surrounded her.

The bakery didn't smell this festive any other time of the year. Eugenia's fruitcakes, which owed their unique flavor to an ancestral recipe, lined the counters and folks were buying. The Branson Christmas Tour buses were starting their annual pilgrimage to The Strip, and occasionally one still turned off the main highway so the passengers could purchase a Jolsen's goodie.

Roni smiled to a neighbor and eased off her shoes. She had written the notice regarding the new position on the town's annual tree. The article would come out in the weekly paper. Folks would be upset. They would miss the spruce as much as she would. Even the thought dampened her spirit, but she wasn't going to let Brisco's cuts upset her. She'd be around long after he was gone. Her gaze shifted to the window, where the light ice coating had dissipated overnight. Today's weather was downright balmy, and she had to admit the fifty degrees didn't add much to her holiday mood. Others seemed unaffected as they hurried by the window.

Roni, you're a sentimental fool. Shake it off. You can't let Brisco ruin your holiday.

Speak of the Devil. Jake Brisco walked by and turned to enter the bakery.

"Be with you in a minute!" Eugenia parroted over a sea of customers.

He lifted a hand in response, his eyes perusing the showcase. Shrinking back in her chair, Roni fumbled for her shoes with her toes. The last thing she wanted was more fiscal cut talk.

When Jake lifted his eyes, recognition flickered.

She smiled.

He smiled back. After a moment, he walked toward her table as the small room filled to capacity.

"Hey."

"Hey," she responded. "Busy place."

Taking a chair, he sat down. "I heard they're making rye bread today."

"You like rye?"

"Love it. How about you?"

"I enjoy it. They make Limpa Rye during the holidays. Ed, my next-door neighbor, likes it, so I always purchase several loaves for him during the season."

"What's limpa?"

He was a rye man. Didn't matter what sort, she decided.

"Swedish rye made with molasses and brown sugar. Better buy two loaves and freeze one if you like it. This is the only time of the year you can depend on Eugenia to have a lot."

"I don't have anywhere to keep an extra loaf. My hotel room only has a tiny refrigerator."

"Oh ... right. Well, I have a large freezer. You're welcome to store an extra loaf there." She could have bitten her tongue off. *Why* had she offered her freezer? Wouldn't she see enough of him in the coming weeks?

"Thanks. Coffee? Soda?"

"No, I'm just waiting my turn. The bakery is almost never this busy this early in the season. Maybe taking down the tree won't spoil everyone's holiday after all." She caught her tongue. "Also, Mimsy will be wondering where I am."

"Mimsy?"

"Mom's cat. I kept her."

He nodded. "Part of the family."

The noise level in the close room increased. Folks vied for fruitcakes and Limpa Rye, chatting happily among themselves. Roni felt she should try to carry on a conversation but decided against the effort.

After a bit, Jake scribbled a note on a napkin and passed it across the table. She glanced at the message. "Are you angry about the tree?"

Reaching for the pen, she scrawled. "I'll miss it." She pushed the paper back to him.

His eyes scanned the note. The paper slid back. "Are you angry?"

"Very." Back.

"What choice did I have?" Back.

This one took a while. What choice did he have? Permit the tree to be knocked down at least once or twice more? According to his estimates, and they were probably accurate, that would lead to a pretty sizeable replacement cost. Should she support tradition or sound judgment? She picked up the pen. "None. You were right. Do I have to like it?" She slid the napkin across the Formica.

He wrote, "You can hate it, but don't blame the messenger."

Eugenia yelled. "Roni! You're up!"

Roni shoved her feet into her shoes and reached for her purse. "My turn."

Nodding, he settled back in the chair.

She purchased two loaves of rye and a fruitcake for Ed Carlson. There hadn't been a Christmas in the past several years that she hadn't brought the ninety-year-old this treat.

Tradition, she conceded with a smile, and turned to see Jake Brisco watching her. She frowned. Something he'd know nothing about.

Thank goodness the bakery didn't have a thing to do with city finances.

Ed Carlson had been married sixty-seven years when his wife, Thelma, had a stroke and died. After that, Roni and her mother had looked after the old gentleman. Roni tried to talk him into moving into an assisted-care facility, but Ed would have none of it. He still got around, albeit in a limited capacity. Tonight it took him almost five minutes to open the front door. He was in his robe and slippers, and Roni guessed that he hadn't dressed all day. A thatch of white hair stood up on the back of his balding head from where he'd rested his neck on the back of his recliner. He squinted through the screen door glass to identify the visitor.

"It's Roni, Ed!"

His hearing was gone as well.

"Who?"

"Roni!"

"Roni?"

"I brought you some rye and a fruitcake!"

"Is it Christmas already?"

Grasping the aluminum handle, she opened the door and eased inside. The house smelled of old man and neglect. A 32-inch TV screen blared in the background.

"What month is it?" Ed asked as he shuffled behind her to the kitchen. "I thought I just ate turkey a day or two ago."

"You did. I'm getting an early start on my Christmas shopping this year." She set the fruitcake and bread on his table, which was littered with dirty chili bowls, open cans of Hormel Beef Stew, and pork and beans. "Where are all the leftovers I brought you?"

He cupped a hand to his ear. "What say?"

"Leftovers! Turkey, dressing, mashed potatoes?"

Casseroles, veggies. She cooked enough for two days at a time, and brought them regularly.

He shrugged. "Haven't seen them."

She opened the refrigerator and caught a bottle of ketchup before it hit the floor. The shelves were stacked with foil-covered dishes dating back several days. "You haven't touched your meals."

With a puzzled expression, he peered over her shoulder. "Why I'll be—I didn't know any of that was in there."

She started to empty the bowls that had been there too long to still be edible, in case he might remember them tomorrow. "Did you keep your doctor's appointment this morning?

"Eh?"

"Doctor's appointment? Did you see the doctor today?"

He shook his head. "Haven't seen him in weeks."

She had offered to drive him to his appointments, but he insisted on keeping his 1985 Cadillac and driving himself. He had a limited driver's license and could not drive more than fifteen miles from home. Most days the car sat in the garage.

Roni dumped leftovers into the trash since Ed didn't have a food disposal. Last Christmas she had finally persuaded him that a microwave was safe and it would not give him a lethal dose of radiation. After a few months he started to use it, saying he didn't figure he had that much time left anyway.

"Did you go to the Community Center for lunch?"

Nodding, he shuffled to the table and examined the fruitcake. "They gave us this little piece of meat that wouldn't fill a hollow tooth, plus a little bit of corn or something and some dry mashed potatoes. I miss Thelma's cooking."

Patting his shoulder, Roni sympathized. "I know it's hard to live alone."

"Yes—you would know that," he said. "Your mom was a good person."

"She was, and I miss her too." Straightening, Roni returned to cleaning the refrigerator shelves. "The new consultant came yesterday."

"Oh? Mary Parson's grandson?"

"Yes. Seems the first casualty is the town tree. You'll read about it in Saturday's paper."

"The Christmas spruce?"

"It's been knocked down twice already, and Brisco thinks it costs too much to keep putting it back up."

"Hang the cost. That tree's tradition. My Thelma loved that spruce."

And she had hit it more than her fair share of times, Roni silently mused. "Apparently Mr. Brisco doesn't agree with us. He feels that if the town is to become financially sound we'll have to make sacrifices. The tree is the first thing to go."

"That's a shame. It won't seem like Christmas without that tree."

"It sure won't." She dumped the last of the leftovers and wiped the refrigerator clean. "Have you had dinner?"

"Nope."

Roni opened the cabinet and scanned the near empty shelves. "You like macaroni and cheese, don't you?"

"Yes, I believe I do."

"Then tonight we feast on macaroni and cheese, rye bread, and for dessert, fruitcake!"

Just let Brisco try and snatch that tradition away.

5

The festive holly that adorned the break room couldn't overcome the uneasy silence the following morning. Members of the ice rink committee fidgeted with foam cups, their jaws set like tenacious pit bulls. It was ten o'clock in the morning, and the thermometer outside the window read sixty-three degrees. Jake stood before the grim faces with anything but zest for what he was about to do.

"As you have probably guessed, we are here to discuss the ice rink."

Logan Stokes erupted first. "The weather will turn. Just give it another day or two."

A woman Jake would not have chosen to tangle with on this or any other issue was next. "The rink should have been up and operating by now—certainly by parade night."

Jake sat back and let the comments fly. So-and-so wasn't on top of the situation. They couldn't start the season with so-and-so sitting on his thumbs. At that point

Mr. So-and-so took objection and pointed out that he was not God and he didn't control the weather.

Jake excused himself during a verbal fray and stepped outside his office to the water cooler. Downing three Advil, he tipped his head and swallowed a cup of water.

A rosy-cheeked Roni came out, fanning her face. She grabbed a cup and filled it with water. "You too?"

"They're an opinionated bunch, aren't they?"

She nodded to the bottle of pain reliever. "Do you have any extra?"

Uncapping the bottle, he dumped two in her hand. "One more."

One more landed.

Downing the tablets, she shook her head, turned on her heel, and walked back into the ruckus. Jake trailed behind.

Arms folded over chests as the two reentered the room. "It's a little late to be deciding against the rink," Logan declared.

"Late, yes," Jake picked up. "And there will be a stiff cancellation fee, but it will be a drop in the bucket compared to actually installing and using the ice. Consider a gazebo talent contest. The facility is large and can accommodate fifty or more. Give local talent a chance to shine. Discover new voices."

The woman shook her head. "That wouldn't be Christmas. We've never done it that way."

Jake looked at Roni. "Any suggestions?"

She mutely shook her head.

Jake dropped a folder on the table. "We're looking for cuts, not expenditures. We need alternatives."

His audience sat stiff as ramrods, judgment fixed. Roni stared at her hands, and he knew he had disappointed her once again, but artificial ice? They had to be kidding.

Roni carried a sack lunch to the gazebo, her gaze fixed on the nearby activity. A dump truck backed up to the town tree, the beep, beep, beep driving a stake through her heart.

Removing a tissue from her purse, she wiped clean the concrete bench and sat down. She could have picked a more heartening place to eat, but she wanted to remember the tree, once resplendent in its glory, now disgraced.

The bucket of a front-end loader lowered, and workmen shoved the spruce into the container and yelled. The lift rose and with one resounding burp dumped a town custom.

"Mind if I join you?"

Brisco. And yes, she did mind. She wasn't feeling the friendliest toward the interloper today, but she moved aside and made a place on the bench for him.

He opened a sack, and took out a cellophane-wrapped sandwich with a tuna sticker.

He's eating tuna from a convenience store vending machine.

Removing the sandwich from his hand, she broke off part of her roast beef and handed it to him.

He flashed a remorseful grin. "Thanks. The selection was between this and egg salad."

Nodding, she poured coffee from a thermos. They ate in silence, in the unseasonably warm noon hour. Both looked the other direction as the dump truck drove off with the holiday tree.

He bit into roast beef, pausing to examine the bread. "Is this brown mustard?"

"Yellow."

"I love yellow mustard. It's hard to get on a sandwich anymore."

Roni hadn't thought about it because she didn't eat out that often, but she wondered if yellow mustard would soon go the way of the town holiday tree. Dumped.

Frustrated and disappointed, she wasn't inclined to make idle conversation. She was starting to think her initial assessment of Brisco was right. Sure he had a job, but what about a conscience? Did he even have one?

Jake broke the silence. "The mayor seems to think that the first cold snap will up the Christmas spirit. He was on the phone with the Springfield weather service when I left the office, to get an updated forecast."

"It'll turn cold," she predicted, more hopeful than confident. She refused to consider otherwise. Then, aware that she was not being very good company, she opened a snack baggie and offered him a corn chip. He eyed the contents. "I gather you're a small eater."

She shrugged. "Now that you've had time to look over the ledgers, do you think you can get the town back on its feet?"

Downing the last bite of roast beef, he smiled. "With the right cooperation." He eyed her cup.

Easing the thermos closer to him, she invited. "Be my guest." Drinking from a thermos wasn't exactly hospitable fare, but she only had one cup. And she wasn't out to impress him with social skills.

"Thanks, but I'll just get something back at the office." Stretching out his legs, his gaze skimmed the park surrounding the gazebo. "It really is a nice town. And you have to admit, the gazebo lights look great."

She didn't have to admit it, but they did. The newly added miniature flashing lights, all in blues and greens, were charming. Workmen were busy lining the outside of the gazebo with the same theme. He must have gotten on the phone early this morning and set the work in motion. "Who came up with the idea to go with green and blue?"

"Tess. We were kicking around some different ideas and she thought that blue and green might be a nice change from the usual multicolored lights." Jake paused, and sat up straighter. "What would you say if I suggested that we skip the ice rink this year and have the children do something special? Last winter I was overseas during most of the holiday and I saw some kids making small tree decorations. Paper shaped like horned cornucopias, tree ornaments — that kind of junk."

"Don't call it junk," Roni interuppted.

"Sorry, I don't share the same mushy sentiments as you."

"Obviously."

They sat in silence until Jake continued, "Someone said the children could take their stuff to area nursing homes. Ever give that any thought? Giving of one's self — isn't that what it's all about instead of sticky sentiment? Local churches could donate time to oversee the project."

"Junk" had been elevated to "stuff." No one could accuse him of being overly syrupy. Roni licked mustard off her fingers. "Tess actually thinks Nativity traditions ought to change?"

Jake shook his head. "Tess and I were just trying to come up with solutions. Even you have to admit that change can be good. And getting the town involved in activities that wouldn't cost an arm and a leg would appease your Christmas spirit and unite the citizens."

Even her? How dare he. She loved and supported her community. She was willing to make needed changes but she didn't have to like them. She wadded up the baggie and stuffed it into her coat pocket, another one of mom's frugal habits. "If you'll excuse me, I have a few errands to run before I go back to work."

"Are you sure?" He sat back, crossed his arms behind his head, and gazed up at the clear blue sky. "We could sit here and try to figure this out. It's a fine day."

Maybe for him. "Wonderful weather for September, but it's December now. What we need is some freezing temperatures so we can enjoy the ice rink." She glanced at her watch. "I really must be going."

"Roni?"

"Yes?"

"Think about my suggestion. The gift of time and effort represents the true meaning of Christmas. After all, God's gift of his Son is what started it all."

So he does have a spiritual side. She reached for her purse. "I'll mention the idea to the mayor. But remember, he's not much for change, especially sudden change, and I'm not sure we can even cancel the rink rental at this late date."

"You talk to him. It can be done."

She left him sitting in the balmy sunlight, enjoying his day.

Or his work. She wasn't sure which.

Stepped on her toes again, didn't you, Jake. He was the bad guy, and he knew she would like him more if he had taken away her yellow mustard rather than her traditions.

Well, old man, you are not here to make friends. He studied Roni as she crossed the street and paused in front of Steil's Hardware. Who needed a sentimental nut in their life? Not him. His gaze shifted to the gazebo area. He imagined the place filled with holiday revelers and children making gifts. Tradition was burying this town, so Roni had to ask what she wanted more, solvency or business as usual.

His gaze retutned to Roni who still stood in front of the hardware store window. He'd seen her stop there on her way home at night. What attracted her attention?

She moved on, and he got up and crossed the street, psychologically sharpening his surgical knife. This afternoon he planned to tackle the annual Christmas parade. The city spent an inordinate amount on floats. Businesses kicked in and did their share, but according to the ledger last year's parade had cost Nativity a lot of money. Many of those former businesses had closed or left to relocate in Branson.

Now, according to his notes, the town was about to spend thousands on an hour-long holiday parade.

❧

Jake Brisco is getting on my nerves. He got rid of the tree. He wouldn't dare mess with the parade or the rink.

As Roni stared at the leg lamp, Aaron's face appeared in the window sporting a knowing grin. Was it that obvious that she longed for that silly lamp? What purpose would the object serve, especially at Christmas? Christmas was a time for celebrating Christ's birth, not fishnet hose. Yet the meaning of the movie classic was clear, at least to her. There was a lesson to learn behind the flagrant commercialism of Christmas; family, warts and all, was one of God's greatest gifts.

Yet truthfully, a hundred and ninety-nine dollars was a stiff price for a good laugh.

Roni walked on, leaving Aaron to shake his head.

Warm air ruffled her hair, and she wondered if the global warming that the experts touted so much was going to interfere in Nativity's holiday. Even more disturbing was the thought digging deeper into her mind every day. If Nativity couldn't remain solvent, it would go the way of so many other small towns. Soon broken windows wouldn't be replaced, and the square would be reserved for roosting pigeons. Once that happened, there would be no need for a city administrator.

Then what?

She would have a choice of selling her house and moving, or making the drive to Branson or Springfield every day for employment. She'd worked for the city since she was old enough to hold a job. What would she do if she lost that security? Her credentials were enough for employment elsewhere, but she was content, even stuck in her ways, here in Nativity. She didn't want to change jobs and start all over. Nativity was home, but the Jake Briscos of the world understood bottom-line profit more than life-long comfort and stability.

Shortly after lunch, Jake answered his cell phone and heard the friendliest voice he had heard in days. He had concluded the meeting with the committee, and eliminating the ice rink had been a fight. And while no one had personally confronted him with blame, there was underlying doubt, hurt, and frustration.

Grandma Mary's voice came over the line. "Hello, dear. I know you're very busy, but I wanted to confirm our holiday plans. You'll join me on Christmas Eve?"

Grandma Mary. Youthful for her age, always well groomed, always with a smile in her voice. He regretted the years he'd spent away from her. The past few holidays they'd connected and Jake kinda liked having a grandma. Mary had heart worries, but she was still a vibrant woman. He'd been so busy that he hadn't gotten out to her place but once, and that had been only a brief visit. The same argument took place: she insisting that she pay Jake for his services to Nativity and he refusing to take a cent. "I wouldn't miss it, Grandma."

"I wouldn't miss it either. You know, dear, I've given quite a lot of thought to your present this year, and I think you're going to like what I've selected."

Presents? He hadn't given the idea any thought. "Come on, Grandma. You know presents aren't important to me."

"Nor to me, but some presents are invaluable."

A tie. Handkerchiefs. Gloves. Jake grinned. He could live without them.

"Jake, dear. How's the work coming along?"

"Not so well, Grandma. I'm afraid your neighbors are set in their ways."

"Now, now," she chided. "You must earn your money, Jake."

"I'm not taking your money, Grandma. How many times do I have to tell you?"

Her tone turned censuring. "I would not have hired you if I thought you were going to be unreasonable about this."

"Okay," Jake agreed, unwilling to get into another lengthy discussion about wages. He wouldn't accept a cent for what he considered child's play. This town didn't stand a chance of survival, and it wouldn't take more than a few weeks to prove it to Grandma. Still, she needed to feel that she could make a difference. Jake stepped into his office and sat down. "Have you got a minute?"

"Of course, dear. Is there something you need?"

"A little perception?" Leaning back in his chair, he relayed his morning. She knew these people. Maybe she could offer advice on closed minds. "The town thinks I'm an ogre."

She laughed softly. She was an amazing woman. Strong, but compassionate. Wise, but not overbearing in her wisdom. She'd told him that Grandpa had been the same; well respected within the community, a man of his word. Jake suddenly realized that Roni shared many of his grandparent's most endearing qualities. Straightforward, and able to endure hardships without folding.

Once he explained his situation, he asked, "You think I should leave the Christmas budget alone?" The town was doomed anyway. He could make all kinds of noises about cuts and sacrifices, but his instincts told him that like so many other small towns in the area, Nativity would someday cease to exist as a business community. Its future was pointed toward becoming a bedroom community for Branson and Springfield.

"Yes, it is a rather perplexing dilemma," Mary mused. "If your grandfather were alive, he'd know what to do. Traditions are a valued part of Christmas, and I do know the town loves its holiday season."

The wistful tone that now entered her voice told Jake that her mind was occupied with the events of a Christmas Eve long ago, memories of a time neither of them enjoyed recalling.

"Roni thinks I'm ruthless."

"Roni?"

"She works in the administration office."

"Oh yes. The Elliot girl."

Grandma admitted that she didn't socialize anymore, not since Grandpa died. But she still loved her town, and she wanted the community to survive. He told Mary a little about the city administrator.

Grandma's voice turned playful. "I'd love to meet her sometime. She sounds delightful."

"She is . . ." Jake paused. "Now don't get any ideas. Before I'm through here, it's likely I'll be stoned or run out of town on a rail." He was fast becoming the most ostracized guy in town. Returning to the original question, he asked. "What do you think, Grandma? Am I being too hard on the town? Honestly, between you and me ..."

Roni paused in front of Jake's doorway on her way to the coffeepot. She hadn't meant to eavesdrop, but his voice came to her. "... the cuts aren't going to matter. The town has too many financial obstacles to overcome. I'll do what I can, but in the end Nativity is probably getting ready to enjoy its last Christmas celebration."

Too many financial obstacles to overcome. Roni closed her eyes to a sudden light-headedness. She'd known — or sensed — that this would be the outcome of Jake Brisco's tinkering, but the knowledge still rocked her.

"Just give the phone to ..." Judy strode past, rolling her eyes at Roni. "Anabelle, give the phone to your older sister. No — don't — Anabelle! *Put* the babysitter on the phone. Right now. *No.* Right now! Is that the sound of the stool flushing? Where's the cat?" She covered the mouthpiece with her hand. "Have you ever had a day when you wished you could volunteer for a one-way ticket to Mars?"

Absently nodding, Roni continued to the mayor's office with papers requiring his signature.

This was one of them.

Jake reached to switch off the radio. Outside the window, the grass actually looked greener than it had been yesterday. Radio and TV weathermen had been ecstatic about the continuing warm spell. Old-timers were grumbling that "winters weren't like this when I was a kid." His eyes searched a clear blue sky for change, but the heavens looked more like May than December.

Turning back to his desk, he studied the miniature town model he'd started constructing. During a brainstorm one morning, he had driven to Branson and visited a couple of craft shops. Before anyone else came to work he had brought in everything he needed for a town model.

"Jake?" He turned when he heard Roni's summons. She stood in the doorway, frowning. "The ice rink committee is back again. Do you want to talk to them?"

Actually he didn't. This meeting wouldn't be any more pleasant than the last one. "Send them in."

She turned, and then turned back. "Perhaps if you took money from the snow removal fund and temporarily shifted it to pay for the rink ..."

"And when it snows and we need money for road clearance?"

"It might not; we've had many years when we got only a smattering." She stepped closer. "This year is starting out very mild. It wouldn't be that hard to move the money. The rink would bring in revenue that could go back into the street maintenance fund."

Shaking his head, he sat down at his desk. "Borrow from Peter to pay Paul."

She grinned. "I haven't heard that old phrase since Mom died."

"It's one of Grandma's favorites." Reaching for a ledger, he scanned the columns. Gravel, ice melt, snowplows, gasoline, manpower. There were ample amounts allotted to cover several good snowfalls, but his job wasn't to move checkers. He was there to balance the long-term budget, not gamble on climate patterns. The weather could turn in a matter of hours. He pitched the book on his desk. "No can do, Roni. The rink is out this year."

Her crestfallen expression didn't help his mood. When she turned on her heel and left, he sat back, steeped his fingers, and studied the miniature town laid out before him. Days like today made him wish that he had followed his dream and remained in the air force. Flying was his love, not spoiling the holidays for a pretty, brown-eyed woman who, if only for a moment, made him consider the cockamamie idea of taking money from snow removal to provide an ice rink.

The committee appeared, and he mentally armed himself for another shoot-out. If their stormy expressions meant anything, he would need a bigger gun.

Around five thirty, Roni glanced up to see Jake leaving his office. The committee had taken up half of his day arguing and he was behind on his paperwork, but the rink was out for this year. The cancellation fee would be minimal compared to the construction itself.

He approached, yawning. "Are you working late too?"

She nodded without glancing up from the computer. "End of the month reports."

She finished the report and pushed a key. In the back room the sound of a printer filled the office.

"Done?"

Gathering her purse and keys, she smiled. "All through. I'll lock up."

"Do you have time to grab a burger with me?"

"Can't. Mimsy is waiting for her dinner, and I need to check on Ed."

"Ed?"

"My elderly next-door neighbor. If I don't watch him closely, he won't eat properly."

"So, we feed Mimsy and Ed and then we'll feed ourselves." He knew he wasn't high on her list of preferred dinner company, but she was a rational thinker. She knew that his decisions were sound.

He trailed behind her, flipping off overhead lights.

"Leave the one on in the mayor's office for a nightlight," she reminded.

After she locked up they started toward her home. "What about your car?"

"I'll get it later. How late does the café stay open?"

"It closed half an hour ago. Do you like Chinese?"

"It's okay."

"Mr. Wong's always open late."

By now they were passing Steil's Hardware. Jake suddenly paused, apparently caught by the window display. "Look at that."

Roni's eyes fixed on the leg lamp, pleased that he'd noticed. "Yeah. I've been admiring it, but it's outrageously expensive."

Jake bent closer to the plate glass window. "Expensive? Seems reasonable to me. I would pay more than thirty bucks in Springfield for a set of sockets like that."

Sockets. She might have known.

෬ා

The mild weather made for a nice outing, but then, Jake noticed that when he was around Roni life tended to be nice. She was good company, fun to be with, even though she made his job more difficult.

A large, black-and-yellow-striped cat waited while Roni opened the back door. With a meow, the feline headed for her. Scooping up the cat, she hugged him warmly, and then set him back on the floor. "I'll only be a minute." She reached for a can opener and opened a small tin of cat food.

Jake's eyes roamed the homey kitchen. It had been years since he'd been in a house that reminded him of his early childhood. Linoleum on the floor, a green Formica table, and vinyl covered chairs; live plants sitting in the kitchen window over the sink. African violets. He'd seen the same plants on his mom's windowsill. Through the doorway he spotted the front room with overstuffed sofas and chairs. Fringed table lamps and family pictures lined the wood-burning fireplace. He'd stepped back into a simpler era, a time when groceries were delivered to your back door and young boys on bicycles threw newspapers onto your lawn. Neighbors sat on front porches at night and visited. He imagined that if he sniffed he could smell pork chops sizzling on a skillet.

"Ready to go?" Roni's voice broke into his musings.

"Ready. The cat's food is starting to look good."

Laughing, she switched a light on over the sink, and they left the way they'd come in, through the back door.

"We'll check on Ed and then be on our way."

"I'm right behind you."

Later, over steaming plates of kung pao chicken, Roni felt the day's tension draining away. She wanted to be mad at the man sitting across from her. Chair-kicking furious. After all, he was stealing her Christmas. But she couldn't summon the emotion. He was only doing what he'd been hired to do, and she didn't envy his work or his judgments.

"This is good," he said, reaching for the soy sauce. "What's with the owner's Spanish accent?"

"Mr. Wong? He watches old westerns. Some days he talks in Spanish, other days he calls you pilgrim, imitating John Wayne. He's delightful."

He replaced the lid on the bottle. "Hey, I have to ask you something."

She knew the question would have nothing to do with her opinions about the recent cuts; she'd found that out the hard way. "Shoot."

"Okay, pilgrim. Is it just me, or has one of us grown two heads?"

"It's you," she confirmed. "You've only been in town a few days, and you're acquiring quite a ... shall we say, reputation?"

"Bad guy," he surmised.

"If we rule out Grinch and Scrooge, I suppose bad guy will be adequate." She bit into a crab rangoon. "Though I've pointed out to several people that it was the town's mistake hiring you before Christmas."

"The theory being that after Christmas I couldn't touch tradition?"

"Not until next year."

"But this year, Nativity would have its holiday."

She thoughtfully studied her plate. "I know we seem very shallow and tied to tradition."

"I hadn't thought much about it, but every look you send my way accuses me of being a calloused, heartless management analyst."

She smiled without looking up. "I haven't openly accused you."

Roni was a tough one to figure out. From Jake's observations, he figured she valued convention as much as, if not more than, the other townspeople, but yet she gave him the least flak. Grandma's earlier phone conversation drifted through his mind. *You'll do what you must, Jake.*

Yes, like Grandpa he'd do his job with the most sensitivity possible, but he would do his job.

It was past ten when Jake walked Roni home, and Nativity's streets were empty. "Is the town always this quiet?"

"Business will pick up after Saturday's parade. Santa comes to town that night." Last year Earl Bentley's grandson parachuted in by air, dressed as the jolly old man with a bag full of toys strapped to his back. The children's round eyes were more rewarding than the small payment the town had given him.

They passed the community church where Roni attended. "Do you sing?"

"Only in the shower," he admitted. "Why?"

"I wanted to invite you to choir. We're practicing for the Christmas cantata. We can always use an extra baritone."

"Tenor."

"Really?"

"Would I fib about a thing like that? Thanks, but you really wouldn't want me there. Even Grandma says I should steer clear of music."

She shook her head. "You're a hard one to figure."

"How so?"

"I know little about you, other than the fact that you're a card-carrying Scrooge."

"What'd you want to know?"

"Well—let's start with your abnormal lack of Christmas enthusiasm."

"Must we? Can't a person enjoy the true meaning of Christmas without all the fuss?"

"Sure, but something's caused you to be the way you are."

"And how is that?"

"Not a sentimental bone in your body."

"Okay."

"Okay what?"

"You want my history. Here it goes. After I graduated from high school, I did a stint in the air force, and then opted out to come home for a while. I enrolled in college, got my masters, and then joined the Patton firm."

"And?"

"And that's my life's background."

"Christmas didn't exist in your life?"

"It came around every twenty-fifth of December."

They passed the hardware store, where the leg lamp still glowed brightly.

"That is looking more tempting every day," he confessed.

She stopped, eyes bright. "You honestly like it?"

Pausing, his gaze scanned the window display. "I think I might." Then he shook his head. "I have enough sockets. Can't even find half the ones I own."

~⚬~

Roni's house came into sight. A lamp glowed in the parlor window. Mom always sat a poinsettia in the front window. She left Roni with lots of traditions. She loved having poinsettias throughout the house, and a large tree decorated with ornaments dating back to both Mom's and her childhoods. Every school year was marked with one of Roni's handmade crafts. The assortment didn't necessarily make for a *Good Housekeeping* tree, but it resulted in a sentimental one.

When she released a sigh, he glanced over. "Something wrong?"

"I was just thinking how much I love decorating this house, but maybe that sentiment isn't so great."

"How so?"

"This old house." Her eyes scanned the two-story structure with a concrete wraparound porch. During the summer, Mom's wicker furniture filled the area. Sometimes folks still sat on the porch on summer evenings and visited. "Sentiment has made me keep the house long after I realized that it's too big for one person and a cat."

"Mimsy."

She nodded. "Maybe that's why I continue to hold on to the relic. Mimsy's getting very old and won't be around much longer. When she goes, I'm thinking I'll put the house up for sale and get something smaller and more economical."

He reached for her hand. "You wouldn't miss it?"

Her heart lunged. A man hadn't held her hand in … she couldn't remember the last time. She managed to find her voice. "Miss high utility bills, poor insulation, rattling plumbing, and the lack of dependable hot water pressure during showers? A little," she admitted. "But they say change is good."

"So, you stayed because of the cat?"

"Yeah, Mom loved Mimsy. It would have been like getting rid of a family member if I'd found her a new home." His hand felt warm and assuring in hers. Was it supposed to feel this way? This man was taking away part of her life.

"How old is she?"

"Ageless. I thought she'd pass years ago, but she's still very healthy." They shared a moment of silence before she spoke again. "I use Mimsy as an excuse for keeping the house, but deep down I think I hold on to it because someday I'd like to fill it with children. Children and laughter. I'm an only child and I've always longed for siblings. I don't know why Mom and Dad didn't have more kids — I never asked and they never volunteered the information, but sometimes I'd hear a wistful tone in Mom's voice when she talked about large families." She turned to look at Jake. "You said you lived with your aunt?"

"Since I was nine. My folks were killed in a car accident."

"Siblings?"

"One sister. She was with my parents the night they were killed. It was Christmas Eve, and they were on their way to Grandma Mary's. I had spent the night before with her, and we'd baked sugar cookies that day, so I wasn't in the car. Jill, my sister, lived for forty-eight hours, but then family made the decision to pull life support."

"It must have been a horrible time in your life."

"It took some time to adjust, and I admit I rebelled for a while. My teen years weren't exactly ideal. Christmas was never the same."

"I know. That's why I cling to tradition."

Reaching the house, Roni broke hand contact, though she realized the walk home had been the best she'd ever experienced. Still, it just didn't feel like Christmas yet. There was no back-slapping "Merry Christmas" when people met on the street. No large, merrily twinkling spruce sitting in the intersection.

Saturday's parade would stimulate the spirit. When the balloon artists, carolers, and concessions offering spiced cider and hot chocolate with a peppermint candy cane showed up, the atmosphere would change. Nativity would come alive with the holiday spirit regardless of Jake's cuts.

"Thank you for dinner."

"You're welcome. Thanks for joining me. The motel room gets pretty monotonous."

"Couldn't you stay with your grandmother?"

"Sure I could, but her house is small and I prefer my privacy." He bent and kissed her, just a touch to her lips, but enough to create a sizeable jolt. She closed her eyes, soaking in the touch. *For heaven's sake, Roni. It was an innocuous peck, not a passionate kiss. The guy's just being nice.*

"See you in the morning."

"Yeah," her fingers absently touched the spot he'd kissed. "I'll be there."

_7_

"Roni, have you seen the parade list?"

"Not recently. Why?"

Judy handed over the file. "Read it and weep. I had been meaning to mention the lack of business interest earlier, but I thought there would be a lot of last minute entries."

Roni scanned the sheet. Participation was way down. "Have you called the ones who usually compete?"

"Just finished the list and everyone I spoke to had the same answer: cutting back, business is down, afraid to spend the extra money. It's too late to do anything now. The parade's coming right up."

"This is bad." Applicants were half of what they were in past seasons. She reached for the phone and dialed the Food Mart. Phil's harried voice came on the line.

"Phil ..."

"Now don't start with me, Roni. I've already told Judy that I ain't got the money to put a float in the parade this year. Celery's gone through the roof, bread and milk are outta sight. I got customers drivin' up to Branson to shop at Lucky Mart in spite of high gas prices."

"But Phil, the parade is a wonderful advertisement . . ."

"Not if you have to shut the door to your business." He clicked off.

"See. I told you," Judy said as Roni hung up. "I've noticed the lights at Neilson's haven't been burning late like they usually do."

"I'll call Steve." She punched in the garage number.

"Yo! Neilson's Garage."

"Steve, put your dad on."

"Is this about the parade?"

"Yes —"

"He won't talk to you, Roni. He's busy fixing a flat. Besides, he already told Judy we aren't putting a float in the parade this year."

"He needs to consider —"

"Hey, I like the floats. You don't need to convince me."

"Then put your dad on."

"He won't talk to you. We don't have the money to participate. No dough. Business is down."

She hung up.

Neilson's Garage was the hub of float assembly. By this time of the year, crews would usually be working late into the night on their entries, their infectious laughter and good-natured banter ringing throughout the town. Nativity was starting to resemble a morgue. If Brisco thought green and blue twinkling lights on an empty gazebo could encourage a spending stampede, he was sadly mistaken. She glanced at his office, where he sat staring at a miniature town. Did he actually think he'd make Nativity solvent by playing a board game? Occasionally he'd move tiny automobiles and tour buses to different locations marked with Santa faces or Mary cradling the baby Jesus. Then he would shift a business to another corner, or remove the used clothing store and set a five-and-dime building in its place. She could not figure out what was going on in his analytical mind as Christmas drew closer and her hometown fought for its dying breath. His boredom was highly evident.

Returning to Judy's statement, Roni admitted, "You're right. It's too late to change the businessmen's minds." She picked up the list and perused the entries which included high school marching bands, the Shriners and their funny little cars, a local children's dance studio, and a convertible carrying Little Miss Merry Christmas. She trusted that this year Santa would arrive on time, riding high atop Nativity's antiquated fire engine. She hoped the driver would not delay the jolly man's appearance by flooding the carburetor like he did two years ago.

"We've got to do something if we're going to save Christmas this year." Judy set a box of paper clips on Roni's desk.

"Dusty Bitterman and I are working on an alternate plan if Brisco goes too far." Dusty called almost every day, intent on salvaging Christmas, but Roni still urged caution. Everything was starting to get complicated, between the season and her growing attraction to Jake in spite of his intent.

"Goes too far? He's already gone too far!" Judy complained.

Tess glanced up from the file cabinet. "Brisco hasn't said anything more about cutting the part-time help, has he?"

Roni sighed. "Stop worrying about your job. If it gets that bad, we'll all go."

The older woman closed the file. "That's what I worry about."

Roni was nervous about the same thing, but she wasn't going to encourage the thought. Change was a fact of life, and as much as she loved this town, she knew from seeing other towns die that the large gobbled up the small. It was life's food chain.

"I know. Why don't we move up the date for the home decorating contest?" Judy suggested. "Everybody looks forward to the townwide lighting, and we might as well take advantage of the mild weather. It can't last forever."

"It can't?" Roni had to wonder, but anything was worth a try. Without the tree and the ice rink, it seemed a foregone conclusion that Branson and Springfield would reap the commercial harvest from Nativity this year. The few retail stores still open were not enough to draw folks to the once active downtown.

Perched on the corner of Roni's desk, Judy turned dreamy. "I know what I'd do with the prize money."

"What would that be?"

"Pay off my credit card. The kid's pharmacy bills have been piling up lately. If this croup doesn't run its course I'm going to pull my hair out."

"What about you, Tess?" Roni dropped a letter in the outgoing basket.

"Buy groceries. December's utility bills leave me depleted, and three hundred dollars would go a long way toward stocking up on essentials."

Judy took a sip from her cup. "Roni, you usually win the contest. What would you do with the money?"

Roni thought of the leg lamp in Steil's window. One hundred ninety-nine dollars. She'd buy that lamp and create her own tradition, which now seemed pretty shallow in view of how Judy and Tess would spend the award money. "I might not win," she pointed out. "The Hakes won last year."

The front door opened and Dusty Bitterman, the friendly, peppermint-toting insurance man, stepped inside the office, dropping candy treats on every desk he passed. He pitched a round disc onto Roni's desk. "Isn't it about time for Santa to come see you ladies this year?"

"If he wears sun screen." Roni removed the wrapper and popped the sweet into her mouth. "How many bags of these things do you go through in a season?"

Frowning, he turned thoughtful. "The amount doesn't matter; it's the kiddies' joy that concerns me."

Judy sucked on her treat. "Better get your glasses changed, Dustbo. We're not kiddies."

He winked. "You are to me. I gave you girls candy when you were still toddlers." He focused on Roni. "Now, we've got some decisions to make. Seems to me we're going to have to come up with our own holiday this year. Put our heads together, get something going. I want to save the town as much as the next guy, but we can't let Brisco destroy our holiday."

Shoving back from her desk, Roni said, "I agree. We were just discussing the parade and how few entries we have this year. We're thinking about changing the date of the decorating contest."

"Can't be too soon for me. When are you thinking of starting?"

"Right away, and have the lighting and judging a week before Christmas Eve. We need to do something to get this town's Christmas spirit rolling."

"Amen!" Dusty said. "I'm going to call Shelia and tell her to have our grandson come over and get the decorations down from the attic." Dusty rubbed his hands together. "Hot dog. The house decorating contest. Brisco can't stop this tradition."

But he could put a severe damper on it, Roni thought.

When the door closed behind a whistling Bitterman, Judy admitted. "I guess age and tradition are subjective. How old is Dusty now?"

"He must be well into his eighties."

"And still doesn't carry a cell phone."

"Are you kidding? That'd only confuse him."

Judy sat back. "Eighties, huh. Still working and as vital as ever. Who'll hand out peppermints when he's gone?"

Roni shook her head. It was a good question. Who would hand out peppermint treats in a ghost town?

Roni walked over and stood behind Jake's chair. He looked up, then set a miniature tour bus down and motioned toward the board. "What do you think of it?"

Uncertain of how to answer, she ignored the question and brought up the subject most on her mind. "Judy suggests that we start the home decorating contest right away, since it looks like the parade is going to be small this year and probably won't generate a lot of local shopping enthusiasm." She eased closer to stare at the board. "What is that?"

"Nativity."

She shook her head. "No it isn't. We don't have a five-and-dime, or an old-fashioned—" She bent closer to read the tiny sign, "ice cream and soda fountain." The best Nativity could offer was The Dairy Dream.

Tipping back in his chair, Jake focused on her. "Tell me more about the decorating idea. Is it usually held about this time?"

"A little closer to Christmas, but if we move it up even a few days it could spark some holiday cheer."

Jake reached for a folder, and she held her breath. Had he noticed the three-hundred-dollar prize? Three hundred dollars was insignificant in the big picture, but no doubt important to Nativity's financial health. His eyes scanned the columns. "The town offers a prize for the contest?"

"Three hundred dollars."

"Is the money necessary?" He looked up. "Why is it obligatory? Surely not for the Christmas spirit. After all, the best things in life are free."

"That's true, and no, the money isn't necessary, but it's—"

"Tradition," he supplied a theme that was starting to sound redundant, even to Roni.

"That and the thrill of competition."

"Competition. You know, my grandpa used to say competition was man's worst enemy."

"Why would he think that?"

"Grandma Mary said his theory was that when two people compete, there's a winner and a loser. We all like to win, and the elation we feel at the time is pleasant. But to have a winner is to produce a loser. If a person loses enough times, he starts to think like a loser. Many a 'loser,' though competent and bright, wears the mental label for the rest of his life. Grandpa would always end by saying, 'We are all winners,' and it serves no purpose to point out the short-comings of any man, woman, or child."

"I hardly think that losing a seasonal contest would mar a person for life."

He smiled. "Maybe not, but according to Grandma, Grandpa was pretty wise. Okay, you can change the dates, but let's have the only prize be the recognition of being the owner of the best-decorated house in town. We save the town three hundred dollars, and we don't emphasize losing over the holiday."

Best decorated house in town. Roni hardly thought the title would help pay Judy's credit card bill or buy Tess's groceries. Still, Jake had a point. As much as she hated to admit it, contests did have a way of inflating or deflating the ego.

Admit it, Roni. Brisco's cuts are starting to wear thin. Such minute expenditures couldn't put a dent in the overall deficit, so why not let the town have its holiday? Chances were there wouldn't even be a Nativity next year.

Or would Jake Brisco still be here to dampen the spirit?

Later, she picked up the phone and called Dusty. When the friendly insurance man answered, she let it pour out. "Dusty, he's not going to let us have the decorating contest."

"Who?"

"Scrooge. Brisco."

"How can he stop us?"

"He won't allow the prize money."

"So?"

Her chin shot up. So what? Jake might not allow the prize money, but that didn't mean they couldn't decorate. Her pulse thumped. "You're right."

The older man chuckled. "It's not hard when you stop to think about it. No one but you can take away Christmas, and you're not going to do that, are you?"

"I'm not." She hung up the phone, jerked her jacket on, and grew a backbone. She *certainly* was not.

_8_

There would have been more attendees if the town had hosted a pigeon fight.

The near empty streets and the few courageous families, mostly parents and grandparents of parade participants, who'd turned out to watch the Christmas parade were pathetic. All day long, thunderstorms that commonly occurred in the spring dampened the spirits of the few who braved the wet weather. Tornado sirens blared midway through the event and marching bands ran for cover, hauling tubas and drums to safety.

Nativity's holiday spirit stunk.

Drenched to the bone, Roni slogged home. Would the decorating contest suffer the same fate as the Christmas parade? Now that Brisco had taken away the prize money, would anyone care enough to swathe their homes in colorful lights?

Piece by piece, Nativity was starting to crumble.

She reached her house and paused. It was still early. The tornado sirens had become silent, signalling the all clear. Somehow, tonight of all nights, she needed a reminder that this was the Christmas season, a joyful time of Santa and Rudolph and presents and love.

Perhaps she would take in a holiday show. The Bald-knobbers, with Joy Bilyeu Steele, her favorite entertainer.

A few minutes later she backed the Volkswagen out of the garage. Sprinkles covered the windshield and thunder rolled across the hillsides. She covered the short distance from Nativity to Branson, driving straight to the Landing, a fairly new addition to the tourist town. Shops, restaurants, and holiday lights created a sense of goodwill. A monstrous silver tree decorated in blue welcomed shoppers.

Heading for her favorite dress shop, she put all of her gloomy thoughts aside. Brisco couldn't kill her spirit. Neither could the rain or even the disastrous parade. Christmas wasn't about things. It was about the birth of Jesus. And somehow seeing happy faces and beautiful decorations helped buoy her spirit.

She walked up and down the strip, peering into windows, browsing the unique clock shop, and assessing original oil paintings. Christmas carols filled the air. Shoppers rushed by with gaily wrapped packages and overflowing shopping bags.

She stopped in The Big Popper and purchased a large bag of caramel corn. On her way back to the car she passed a jewelry store. Pausing to admire a necklace, her gaze lifted and none other than Jake Brisco was standing at the glass counter. Swallowing her recent bite of caramel corn, she backed away, hoping to avoid a meeting. She was starting to enjoy his company, which didn't make a bit of sense, but tonight being alone seemed desirable. True, he was personable and had remarkable business savvy, but she shouldn't be drawn to a man who was systematically taking apart her town.

She turned and hurried on, but seconds later Jake's voice called out. "Roni?"

Whirling, she smiled. "Jake?"

"Wait up." He strode down the walk carrying a wrapped jewelry box. "Why aren't you at the parade?"

"It was rained out."

"No kidding?"

"It didn't rain here?"

"Not a drop. A lot of thunder and lightning, but no rain."

It made sense. Nativity was under a storm cloud that refused to lift. She sighed. And why had he skipped the parade? Didn't he have an ounce of civic pride? "So, what brings you to the Landing?"

"Christmas shopping."

"How nice." Of course, Nativity could use the revenue, but admittedly there wasn't a jeweler in town.

"Grandma likes brooches. I've bought her a different piece every year for the past few years, but I wonder if she doesn't get tired of the same old same old."

"A woman can never have too much jewelry." Roni extended the sack of caramel corn. "Want some?"

"Thanks." He took a sizeable handful. "Have you had dinner?"

She lifted the sack of corn. He smiled. "Have you eaten a decent meal today?"

"Mmm ... no. I went to the parade, and when it was rained out I decided to come here."

His gaze searched the scenic area. "Where's a good place to eat?"

This was a really bad idea. Soon Jake would be gone, and most likely so would she. He'd come around every so often to see his grandma, but a door would close on their relationship. They would no longer see each other every day, and the relationship would fizzle out. Common sense told her that Nativity couldn't exist much longer; the dismal holiday season would be the final blow. Tears welled to her eyes, and she blinked back the telling moisture. "I'm really not hungry."

"Then sit with me while I eat. I haven't had a thing since breakfast."

They were approaching Garfield's, one of her favorite places to eat. *Why not, Roni? Why not take advantage of a pleasant reprieve?*

"Here's one of my favorite restaurants."

Opening the door, he motioned for her to step inside. At this late hour, empty tables were available.

"How many?" the hostess asked.

Jake smiled. "Two. And could we have a table outside?"

"Absolutely. Follow me."

Roni found herself in front of Jake, trailing the waitress outdoors where tables with umbrellas sat along the railing next to Lake Taneycomo. Tonight, gentle temperatures made Jake's outdoor seating preference ideal. The sky cleared overhead, and a soft breeze blew off the water.

Drawing a deep breath, Roni settled into her chair and allowed the Christmas spirit to saturate her. Carols played softly in the background. Lights shimmered off the placid water. Jake was sitting across from her. What started out as a disappointing evening had suddenly turned very pleasant.

After orders were placed, Jake settled back in his chair, his eyes fixed on her. "I figured you wouldn't be speaking to me."

"I ..." There was no purpose in misleading him. She had been upset about him taking the home decorating prize money away this year. There had to be a limit to his cutbacks. To her, the three-hundred-dollar prize had almost been the last straw. "I was upset. Still am, but I can't say that I don't understand your decision. But I don't have to like it."

"Neither do I," he confessed. "If I'd known this particular assignment would be so difficult I would have turned it down."

She glanced up. "Seriously?"

"Seriously. Do you think I like making the cuts I've made?"

"It isn't a matter of 'like.' It's your job to make cuts."

"Precisely. I hope you understand my position."

The waitress arrived with their drinks and set the glasses in front of them. In spite of her earlier "not hungry" response, Roni couldn't pass up deep-fried mushrooms and a Diet Coke.

"Let me guess," Jake said as the waitress left. "You're thinking, 'But why the decorating contest? Three hundred dollars is nothing.'"

She stifled the urge to send a paper missile in his direction as she removed the straw wrapping. "Correct so far."

"This Brisco guy's a jerk."

"Keep going." She grinned and stuck the straw in her drink.

His features sobered. "I know it seems that way, but three hundred dollars here, four hundred dollars there—it all adds up, and while I value the meaning of Christmas as much as the next person, my real joy will be putting Nativity back into the black."

She couldn't argue with logic, yet could a price be fixed on people's traditions? "Money isn't everything."

"No, but to Nativity it's a means of existence. Too many small towns in this area have fallen victim to changing circumstances. I want to see Nativity thrive."

Toying with her straw, she admitted. "If we're speaking candidly, then I have to admit that I believe it's too late to save the town. Our economy has been so dreadful the past few years. The town has nothing to offer. Now, with the recent cuts, people have lost heart. I hear it everywhere I go. The citizens know their little town won't last much longer."

"What did Nativity offer when the buses used to come through?"

She shrugged. "The Dairy Dream was the biggest draw. They serve the largest cones in the county. Folks seemed to enjoy the small-town atmosphere. While they ate their cones they'd browse the stores. We had a novelty shop that carried Christmas ornaments with the town stenciled on front, and some would buy Christmas cards and address them. Every store had a collection box, and the next day the owners would carry them to the post office where Nadine, our postmistress, would postmark them

'Nativity.' Then she would mail them all on the first day of December.

"The tour people were also drawn to the house decorations. Nativity is known throughout the area for our festive celebration and the way the town goes all-out for the event. The day of our annual lighting, folks from out of town would come in for the whole day. They'd eat, shop, and ice skate. Then everyone would stay to see every house in town lit at the same time."

"Fun idea," Jake responded. "I rarely visited Grandma after the accident, especially at Christmas, so I never saw the lighting event."

Roni sighed. "Nadine always looked forward to this time of year, but this season she's worried we won't have enough mail to justify keeping a post office."

Jake listened intently, stopping her occasionally to ask questions. Their food arrived, and they talked between bites. "Did you have a big Christmas when you were a kid?"

Nodding, Roni dipped a mushroom into her tub of ranch dressing. "I'm an only child, but my mom came from a large family. My aunts and uncles live in Kansas City, but over the holidays they all came to our house. The place would overflow from Christmas Eve until New Year's Day, when they'd all pack up their gifts, luggage, dogs, and kids and leave." She took a cautious bite of the hot mushroom. "What about you?"

"My holidays were pretty quiet after the accident. My aunt wasn't one to decorate or make a big fuss, and I was a disagreeable teenager. I never wanted to come and visit Grandma Mary during the holidays. I still don't make a fuss. I'm usually home and in bed by ten o'clock."

Roni smiled. "That's a shame. You've missed a lot."

He shrugged. "Occasionally I think back and realize that having a big family would have been nice."

"Big families have their drawbacks too. They can get awfully loud. How long did you live with your aunt after the accident?"

"Until I went into the air force."

"How long were you there?"

"I opted out after four years."

"You didn't enjoy the service?"

"No, it wasn't that. My first love is flying. I have a pilot's license, and I was training to fly missions in Iraq, but I have this sense of duty that plagues me. My aunt passed away, and Grandma Mary had a heart attack. There wasn't much family left in the area, so I decided to come home and look after Grandma. It wasn't all bad." He winked. "I found out she makes a mean meatloaf at Christmas."

"Meatloaf? You don't have the traditional turkey?"

He shook his head. "Meatloaf. There's nothing better. Meatloaf and raisin pie. After our Christmas Eve dinner, she sends the leftovers home with me. I warm them up and have them on Christmas Day while I watch the football games."

Roni gave him a condescending look. "You watch football on Christmas?"

"As much as possible. I look forward to it every year."

"What happens if cable goes out that day?"

He glanced up. "Perish the thought."

"It could, you know." The lights had, in essence, gone out in Nativity.

"Honestly? I don't know what I'd do. It would spoil the holiday." Then he got the connection. "But cable and town expenditures are two different things."

"Perhaps." For him. She bit into a mushroom.

Later, Jake walked her to the Volkswagen. Once she was seated and buckled up he bent in and kissed her. When he was about to lift his head and break contact, she impulsively brought him back with both hands. As the kiss deepened, she knew she was in deep water, as vast and unknown as beautiful Lake Taneycomo.

Roni set a tiny cradle in the window of the advent calendar on her desk, thinking of all the activities she'd yet to start, primarily putting up her house decorations. When Jake eliminated the prize money, most families in town had rebelled. Childish attitudes prevailed as the homes in Nativity sat dark with only a lighted Christmas tree in the window. Even Roni was guilty of mutiny. She'd begun to think like the others. Why go to all the trouble? If everyone's house looked like it did every other month of the year, why should she knock herself out dragging down all those decorations from the attic? Dusty insisted they implement their own plans, but she still held off. Her heart just wasn't in Christmas yet.

"I'm going to the post office!" Roni called to Judy, who was in the back room.

"Okay!"

"Need anything?"

"Bring me back a large soda with lots of ice."

Temperatures had finally settled into a more seasonal pattern. Huddled deep into her wool coat, Roni crossed the street. Nadine was behind the counter when Roni entered the post office.

"Morning, Roni."

"Good morning, Nadine. I need stamps."

"Sure thing." The woman slid off her stool and opened a drawer. "I suppose you want holiday ones?"

Roni perused the possibilities, and chose the large red poinsettia. "Fifteen will be enough."

"Fifteen it is." Nadine began counting out the purchase. "You know, there was a time when I couldn't keep these stamps in stock this time of year." She shut the drawer. "Things sure have changed."

"No one brings their mail here for the Nativity postmark?"

"A few locals still want it, but even that's slowing. In case you haven't noticed, local Christmas spirit has disappeared."

Roni laid a twenty on the counter and found herself defending Brisco. "I know Jake is working hard to correct the town deficit."

"Might be, but talk is, he's the problem."

"You know that isn't fair. He's just doing his job."

She hooted. "And we're going down like a lead sinker."

Picking up her change, Roni gave the postmistress a harsh look. "It's hardly rational to blame a man for doing his job."

Nadine sobered. "Oh girl, you haven't gone and fallen for the guy, have you?"

"Don't be silly." Roni closed her wallet. "Can't a person defend someone without being accused of falling for him?"

"I hear you two are awfully close."

"Well, you hear wrong. By the way, I'm supposed to tell you that the date for the church cantata has changed."

"Changed? What's wrong? Brisco can't cancel the cantata."

"Jake wouldn't even think of—" She caught her aggravation. "The choir director decided that since so many families are planning on being out of town this holiday that the Saturday night before Christmas isn't suitable for the concert."

"When is suitable?"

"Thursday night."

"*Thursday* night." Nadine shook her head. "I've never heard the likes. They haven't changed the Christmas Eve service, have they?"

Roni sent another censuring look. "Of course the Christmas Eve service is still on."

"Just wondered. I thought Brisco might have decided to cancel that too."

"Don't be absurd. He has nothing to do with the church program."

"It's a good thing, or else—"

Roni rudely closed the door behind her and blocked Nadine's complaint. A cold wind swept the pavement, skipping leaves along the sidewalk.

Crossing the street, she caught sight of the China Wok. Mr. Wong had set a small, but gaily decorated tree outside the establishment. At least he'd caught the spirit. The holiday reminder drew Roni. Though it was barely eleven o'clock in the morning, she suddenly craved sweet and sour chicken.

She entered the welcoming restaurant on a gust of wind. Mr. Wong glanced up from behind the counter and broke into a grin. "Senorita Roni!"

Spanish today, Roni noted. "Are you serving yet, Mr. Wong?"

"Si. Sit." He motioned to the rows of empty tables, each with a festive poinsettia sitting in the middle.

Roni picked the one closest to the window, where she could stare at the twinkling tree. Outside, the wind blew power lines in a frantic dance. Inside the restaurant, Christmas carols floated softly over the speakers. Other than the night that she and Jake had eaten beside Lake Tanycomo, she hadn't felt so festive this season.

Focusing on the flashing lights, she sipped the hot tea Mr. Wong brought. The steamy liquid warmed her insides.

She sat up straighter when she saw Jake leave the city office in a big hurry. Still pulling his jacket on, he strode to his car and the lights blinked when he hit the unlock button.

"Mr. Wong!"

The owner peered around the kitchen doorway. "Si?"

"I'll be right back."

"Okay by me, pilgrim." He disappeared around the corner.

Roni realized that she should have worn her coat as she crossed the street. Jake was pulling out of the parking spot in front of the office. She waved him down.

"Where are you going in such a hurry?"

"I just got a call from St. John's Hospital. Grandma's taken ill, and they've transported her to Springfield."

"When?"

"Evidently several hours ago. My cell had been on the charger."

"Is there anything I can do to help?"

"Ride to Springfield with me."

It only took seconds for Roni to go back for her coat and purse, and to cancel her order.

"Oh—and Mr. Wong?"

"Si?"

"Would you please deliver a large Dr Pepper with extra ice to Judy?"

He nodded agreeably. "I'll mosey right over."

Roni paid him and then put on her coat and left. Moments later the silver Acura sped away.

St. John's hospital complex commanded most of the corner of National Avenue and Cherokee Street. Roni recalled how when she was a child she loved to visit the facility and see the nuns dressed in black, their gowns whispering down the silent corridors. Once, a sister had taken Roni into her office and written on a small card, *God bless Ronda Lucille Elliot.* That card was still tacked to her bedroom wall. When life got tough, Roni would look at the message and remember the sister's kind face, and feel better.

Mary was still in the emergency room when they got there, but she was resting comfortably. The doctor told Jake that his grandmother had a mild cardiac episode. Serious, but not critical. From her cubicle, Mary gave Jake a smile and a "thumbs-up" sign.

Soon after their arrival she was moved to a private room. The doctor could say little more than that she was aging and the heart condition was persistent.

They stood in the hallway until the nurses left and gave them permission to visit her. Roni trailed Jake into the room where the small, frail-looking woman lay on the bed.

"Comfortable?" Jake asked softly.

"Jake? Are you still here?"

Roni slipped quietly into a chair, not wanting to interfere with Jake's ministry.

"Of course I'm still here. Why is the room so dark, Grandma?"

"Why ... because nobody's opened the blinds." The sense of humor indicated a mind and spirit still active and alert.

"I'll take care of that." Jake drew the curtains and daylight illuminated the room. Stepping back to the bed, he reached for her hand. "What's going on here? You're not allowed to be sick."

She was able to achieve a feeble, but sincere, smile. "I'll get sick if I want, Jake Brisco."

He reached behind him and pulled Roni up and close to the bed. "Grandma, this is Roni Elliot."

"Roni." Mary reached for her hand. "The Roni you've spoken about."

Jake had told his grandmother about her? Roni glanced at him, but he was focused on the woman in the bed. "The nurses say you're doing well."

"Do they?"

"We can't have you sick here during the holidays."

She offered another weak smile. "No, that won't do at all." She suddenly caught his hand closer, fervor burning in her eyes. "Jake ..."

"Shhh, Grandma. You're going to be fine."

"Jake, I've failed you."

"You're talking nonsense, Grandma. Now rest."

She laid back, her breath short. "We should never leave unspoken ... the things that need to be said."

Jake attempted to calm her, but she pushed him away. "No. This needs to be said. When your parents and sister ... were killed, I allowed my pain to shape your life. I should have taken you in, raised you, and given you a sense of true family. I was overwhelmed with ... bitterness and misery, and when the holiday approached I'd draw into a shell and pray that the weeks would pass quickly ... so we'd be done with hurtful reminders. I knew you never wanted to come see me, and God forgive me, I didn't insist that your aunt bring you here. Never once did I consider the good that remained in my life."

Nudging a blanket aside, Jake perched on the edge of the mattress. "Don't blame yourself. I never wanted to come. I was a kid who had better things to do, or so I thought."

Mary suddenly changed the subject. "Your mother hated meatloaf, did you know that? She refused to eat it as a child."

"I think I've consumed her share the past few years."

She patted his hand. "Do you recall the fun and laughter Christmas used to bring?"

"Sure I do, Grandma. I couldn't wait for Christmas Eve at your house, especially the cookies we'd bake."

"Such warm memories. I'd decorate every nook and cranny of the house. Your folks would come for the holiday, and your mom and I would make pies and candy. Those were some of the best times of my life, and your Aunt Louise deprived you of such memories. After the accident, my Christmases were so quiet; so very silent."

"Grandma, you're going to be around for many more Christmases, and if you want to decorate the house this year, I'll help."

Roni said softly. "I'll help too. The nurses say you're doing remarkably well." She didn't know why she felt an instant bond with this woman. Maybe it was because she reminded Roni of her Grandma Sue. Grandma used to phrase her speech in the same odd, broken pattern.

"Wouldn't that be lovely." Mary's eyes drifted shut and she laid still. Roni glanced at Jake, who bent closer to check her breathing.

"She's asleep," he whispered.

"I'm not asleep, Jake. I'm only catching my breath. I'm so tired. There's so much I want to tell you. I should have mailed you the lamp. I should have at least done that much."

"You did, Grandma. Several years ago."

"I did? Silly me. I guess I wanted to forget it." Mary blindly groped for his hand. "I didn't get a chance to feed Max."

"I'll stop by and feed your dog, Grandma."

"Give him a little extra tonight," she whispered. "He cried when I left in ... the ambulance."

10

Rush hour traffic packed National Avenue when the Acura pulled out of the hospital drive. Roni longed to erase the worried lines etching his forehead. "I know you're concerned, but the nurses say she's doing very well."

"She looks frail to me." Jake reached for Roni's hand. "I don't know what I'd do without her. It took a long time to form a relationship, but we did. She's all I have now."

Roni tightened her grip in his. "God willing, you still have lots of time with your grandma."

"Do you mind if I stop by my place, and then feed Max? I want to pick up a few things."

"Not at all. I'm in no hurry."

Besides, Jake was growing on her. She'd love to see how and where he lived his personal life.

Jake's residence was the entire second floor of a building that had once housed Springfield Grocer Company.

The structure sat on Booneville Street near the hub of Springfield's downtown area, the historic, old town district where second and third floor spaces were being refurbished into trendy lofts and apartments. When the Acura pulled up in front of the building, Roni couldn't contain her excitement. "This is where you live?"

"This is it." Jake cut the engine, got out, and opened her door.

To the left was a private elevator that whisked them to the second floor. The bottom floor was empty with a *For Lease* sign displayed prominently.

"You're renting out space?" Roni asked.

"The building's too big for one family. It was once a wholesale food distribution operation." He sniffed. "If you have a good imagination you can still smell the aroma of fresh ground coffee."

Drawing a deep breath, Roni detected the faint fragrance. "You really can."

The elevator stopped, and she stepped out into the apartment itself. Jake flipped a switch and soft lighting lit the luxurious area. The apartment had a marble entry, plush sofas and chairs, and rich mahogany tables; carpets and accessories from abroad filled the spacious loft.

"It's breathtaking," she murmured.

Jake walked through the room switching on additional lighting. "When I was a kid I used to come here around the holidays. My parents knew the owners then, and Jill and I would sit in the front window and watch the Christmas parade. It was quite an event back then. If I were lucky I'd get to invite a friend from school, so I became pretty cool around Christmastime."

"I'll bet you were cool all the time."

"I wasn't," he assured her. "I was a geek with big glasses. I wore sweaters and slacks. I ate lunch alone every day, except for the couple of weeks prior to the holiday parade." He hit a button and the drapes drew back to reveal downtown Springfield. "Several years ago, the old building came up for sale and I bought it." He motioned. "Come here."

She walked over to enjoy the sight. Outside, Christmas lights were starting to come on. The neon signs and the lighted snowflakes hanging from the streetlights glistened and glowed. The sight gave her goose bumps.

Jake's arms encircled her waist, and she leaned back to rest against his tall frame. "Pretty, isn't it?"

"It's lovely."

Then his tone sobered. "Do you think Grandma will make it?"

How she wished she could remove the worry in his voice. A cardiac episode could be serious. The nurses had said she was stable, but anything could happen at her age. "I don't know, Jake. All we can do is pray."

He squeezed her waist and then released her. "The attic's this way."

"The attic?"

"Yeah, I have to look for something. Want to help?"

"Sure."

She turned to follow him through the spacious apartment. Pausing in front of a door, he confessed. "It's probably cluttered up there. I've been promising myself I would clean it, but I haven't gotten around to it yet." He opened the door and ushered her up a steep flight of stairs.

The attic area was monstrous. Stored items dating back to the days that the building had been a food company met her eyes. Coffee grinders, huge barrels that had once held coffee beans, counters, light fixtures. The faint smell of coffee lingered here too.

"This junk was part of the deal," he explained. "Nobody's ever wanted to move it, so it's stayed over the years." He paused, his eyes searching the dimly lit space. "The Christmas decorations should be over here somewhere," he said, leading the way through a maze of piled boxes. After a bit of searching, they struck gold. They located a section marked "Christmas." Standing back, Jake shook his head. "I haven't touched this stuff in years. It might take a while to find the lamp."

"You're looking for a lamp?"

"A very special lamp."

His prediction was accurate, as it took a lot of digging to locate the item, but the search produced priceless memories for him. He held up an ornament he'd made in first grade. "Did I mention that I'm an artist?"

The dried glue and sequined angel made Roni laugh.

He frowned. "You're laughing at Picasso-quality work?"

She bit her lip to stop the laughter. "It's very ornate."

One box after the other exposed ornaments, tinsel, lights, and half-melted candles. Finally Jake hit pay dirt. "Wait. I think I've found it."

She scooted closer. "Open it. I can hardly wait to see what we've been looking for."

His expression softened when he lifted the ornate porcelain base and held it up for inspection. "It's exactly as I remember."

Roni examined the exquisite pattern. "It's so very lovely. Was it your mother's?"

"No, Grandma took it out of her front window on the night of the car accident. She never put it up again. A few years ago she sent it to me, but I stored it away."

Handing it back, Roni smiled. "It's very unique, like your grandmother."

Cold sunlight backlit the treetops early the next morning when Jake drove back to Springfield. He grabbed a cup of gas-station coffee and headed for the hospital. A quick call when he got up assured him that Grandma had spent a comfortable night. Sleep had eluded him. He'd tossed and turned, trying to figure out why Christmas no longer held the meaning it once had. Sure, without Mom, Dad, and Jill, nothing was ever the same. But life had gone on.

The family wasn't a stranger to trouble. The year Mom fell and broke her arm, she'd been in a cast all summer. Dad had run the household. The year Grandpa died cleaning out a hedgerow had put a pall over the family. For years Jake had heard his parents talk about how bad things had been when Dad had gone without work for a year and a half after Jake was born.

Half an hour later, the Acura wheeled into the hospital parking lot. Jake walked towards the entrance, balancing a flower vase and a cardboard box. Frost glistened off the sidewalks.

The fourth-floor corridor was quiet. It was early; the morning shift was just coming on duty. Nurses finished their charts, and the rattle of breakfast carts broke the sleepy silence. When Jake stepped into Mary's room he saw that she was still sleeping. The nurse rose, lifting her finger to her lips. He stepped back into the hallway and the nurse followed. "Mr. Brisco. I didn't expect to see you this early."

"I forgot something that Grandma needed."

"She's resting peacefully. I'll take whatever you've brought and give it to her when she wakes."

"Thanks, but I want to deliver it myself. I won't disturb her, I promise."

Moving back into the hospital room, Jake eased to the window where he quietly lifted the blind enough to set the bouquet of roses on the shelf. Then carefully, he set the box on the floor and removed the hurricane lamp and plugged it in. Soft light encompassed his grandmother's sleeping form.

Stepping back, he drank in the familiar sight. He'd forgotten how pretty and comforting the lamp was. Perhaps, as Grandma had reminded him, there were other things he'd overlooked the past years.

Turning around, he bent down to gently kiss his grandmother's forehead, and murmured softly, "Now it's Christmas, Grandma."

"Yeah. I'm taking a mental health day."

Judy's sleepy voice came over the phone line. "Are you sick?"

"No, I just need a day off so I can stay sane." Roni spoke around a light clip between her lips. "Actually, I feel better than I've felt in months." She secured a string of lights to the gutter. "Tell Jake and the mayor I'll be back tomorrow."

"Okay," Judy acknowledged. "You know I hate it when you're not there. It's like a tomb in the office."

"I'll be back tomorrow," Roni promised, and clicked off.

Balancing on the ladder, she punched in Dusty Bitterman's number. When he answered she said, "Alert the troops."

"Hot dog! It's about time." He hung up.

Wedging the phone into her jeans pocket, she then wrapped a couple of light strings around her arm and checked to make sure the staple gun was still hooked to her belt. She agreed with Jake's grandma: Christmas was a little overdue this year.

A steady "snap, snap, snap" filled the crisp morning air as she set to work on the roof. Tiny snowflakes swirled around her as she secured the strings of bulbs to the house fascia. The weather had finally gotten with the game plan.

Ed Carlson wandered out onto his front porch. His hair stood straight up as if he'd just climbed out of bed. "What's going on?" he called.

"Putting up my Christmas decorations, Ed!"

She stapled a string of lights to a shingle. As she worked, neighbors' doors opened and sleepy folks appeared, carrying huge boxes that they set beside their homes. Men dragged ladders out of garages, and before long a crowd assembled below Roni. Willing hands held the ladder steady and stood ready to hand her anything she needed. Women brought thermoses of hot coffee to the growing crowd and the atmosphere took on a holiday feel.

By eight o'clock a few people broke away to go to work, but the sound of staplers and squeaky ladders continued. Nativity had found their spirit. Up and down the street, lights went up and the sound of Christmas filled the cold snowy air. Fake snowmen appeared in yards, accompanied by bogus reindeer. Inflated plastic snow globes blowing synthetic snow took shape.

The fury continued by flashlight into the night, when people came home from work and were caught back up in the frenzy. By noon the following day, decorations were starting to pop up all over town.

"You and Bitterman finally did it." Judy grinned when Roni walked into the office the next morning.

"No, the town did it. Dusty and I only encouraged them to recapture the spirit."

"Regardless, it's turned into a holiday frenzy."

"Do you think Jake's noticed?"

Judy's jaw dropped. "Noticed? Everybody's noticed. I saw a decorated tree sitting next to the road on my way in this morning."

"Not a cent is coming out of the town coffers," Tess reminded. "And I for one am thrilled that folks have caught the spirit. It hasn't been Christmas until now."

"Why Tess," Roni teased, "I thought you agreed with Jake's cuts."

"I do. He's sharp as a tack, but that doesn't mean that I don't love Christmas."

Roni shook her head. "I hope Jake feels the same. He's honestly trying to help."

Judy shrugged. "He's never suggested that we couldn't celebrate Christmas, and besides, he's not here."

Roni glanced at Brisco's desk. "Where is he?"

Judy bent to her work. "He took the next couple of days off to be with his grandmother."

Pulse quickening, Roni asked, "Is she worse?"

"I don't think her condition has changed, but he felt he should be with her. He left you a note on his desk."

Roni walked over and located the white envelope marked with her name. Sitting down in Jake's chair, she read the brief message:

Roni,

I've decided to sit with Grandma for a couple of days. If I don't see you before Christmas, I hope you have a blessed holiday. I trust I haven't ruined it for you or the others in Nativity.

Jake

Folding the paper, she slid it back into the envelope. Ruined her holiday? Actually, he had improved it. She was brimming with Christmas cheer, and it was all because of a simple hurricane lamp. Life was precious, and it didn't take a boatload of money or the idea that "we've always done it this way" to make the holiday meaningful.

Outside the window, Nativity sprang to life. Once the fever spread, the citizens had taken over. Christmas Eve was two days away, and everyone seemed bent on catching up from a late start. Word spread of plans for a townwide holiday celebration after the church's candlelight services on Christmas Eve. Those who had planned out-of-town trips were now grumbling.

Stepping to the window, Roni focused on the harried activity. Wreaths hung in every business pane. Folks scurried past the office with wrapped presents under their arms. Across the street, a group of volunteers decorated a large cedar, not in the intersection, but on the sidewalk near the entrance to an alley. They anchored the top to the walls of nearby businesses, so it wasn't as professional and sturdy as the usual spruce, but it only had to stay erect a few days. She'd heard talk that church members were going from house to house gathering decorations for the tree. Her gaze shifted to the gazebo area, where a team of Veterans of Foreign Wars was setting up folding tables for spiced cider and hot chocolate.

Turning from the window, her eyes caught the miniature town replica that Jake played with. The community didn't look much like the present Nativity. What did he have in mind? Bending closer, she focused on the buildings, the tour buses, and the obvious Christmas theme. If he was taking Christmas away from Nativity, he certainly had an odd way of doing it.

Roni's cheeks warmed when she thought about the hour they'd spent in the attic in search of the hurricane lamp. Jake had been different—almost sentimental. A smile escaped her. There was hope for that man. Then she sobered. Once he saw the town and its Christmas excesses would he feel that she had the same mind-set?

Her thoughts turned to the sound of the front door opening. Dusty Bitterman breezed in, dropping peppermints on desks. "Merry Christmas!"

Judy and Tess already had the candy in their mouths when Roni straightened to catch the piece Dusty pitched her.

"Happy holidays, young lady!"

"Dusty, I don't know what we'd do without you." Roni unwrapped the cellophane and stuck the candy in her mouth.

A grin encased the insurance man's cheerful features. "Have you ever seen such holiday spirit? It just makes you feel good to be a part of it."

Tess started on the daily mail. She picked up an envelope and slid the opener beneath the seal. "It sure does. I understand we have you and Roni to thank for all this last minute activity."

Dusty sent a wink in Roni's direction. "We've had a few talks."

Tess suddenly paused. "Why this is addressed personally to me? It's not shaped like a Christmas card." She read the paper, frowned, and then read it again.

Her puzzled look caught Roni's attention. "Something wrong, Tess?" She sat down at her desk.

"Someone's made a mistake. This letter says I've won a three-hundred-dollar gift certificate at the Grocery Mart."

"Wonderful!" Judy and Roni said in unison.

"Now that really makes it Christmas," Bitterman added.

"But it can't be right. I didn't enter a drawing at the Grocery Mart."

"Maybe someone entered for you?" Roni reached for a file folder.

"Did you?"

"No. I didn't know Grocery Mart was having a drawing." Roni glanced at Judy. "You're in there more than I am. Did you enter?"

"I didn't enter, but I would have if I had known."

"Strange." Tess laid the paper on her desk.

"Don't look a gift horse in the mouth," Judy murmured. "If you can't use the prize, I sure can."

"I can use it. It will see me through the winter months. I just don't understand how I won if I didn't enter."

Tess continued sorting through mail. "Judy, you got mail too." She handed the letter off to Judy.

"Oh drats. The pharmacy bill. I wonder why they sent it here? This and Christmas expenses are going to eat us alive." She tore into the envelope.

"Where's Brisco?" Bitterman asked.

"He's sitting with his ill grandmother for the next couple of days."

"What a shame. And here at Christmastime."

Judy let out a yelp. Heads swiveled. Her mouth was moving but nothing came out.

"What?" Roni half rose out of her chair. "Did someone die?"

Judy waved the pharmacy bill, speechless.

Roni's heart went out to her. Three children to feed, clothe, and buy medicine for. Utility bills were so high this time of year, plus the added holiday expenses. Judy's emotional display seemed to indicate bad news.

"Don't worry. I'll help out—"

Judy found her voice. "It says here I have a hundred dollar credit."

"Credit?"

Judy's expression deflated. "It's a mistake, of course. But boy, for a minute there I was on cloud nine."

Dusty unwrapped a peppermint and stuck it in his mouth. "Why not just sit there and enjoy the comfort for a moment."

"Sorry Dustbo, but it has to be a computer error." Judy sighed. "I owe at least two hundred or more. It's been a terrible month, with the kids being sick and all."

"Well, you just never know," Dusty contended. "After all, this is the season of miracles." Judy and Tess both looked up.

Roni suddenly caught the significance of Dusty's words. The man was pure gold. An angel. Regardless of the town's precarious situation, he had paid Tess's grocery bill and Judy's pharmaceutical nightmare. And though no one would ever know for certain, she'd bet he'd paid Brisco's wages to save the town. Once Tess and Judy had time to think about it, she was sure they would reach the same conclusion.

"Dusty's right, ladies. It is the season of miracles. You know ... angels singing to shepherds, a virgin giving birth, and wise men from the east."

When the door closed behind the insurance man Tess glanced at Roni. "Do you think he entered me in the drawing?"

"Nope. I don't think he did." The prize had come straight from Dusty Bitterman's heart and bank account, the same way Judy's pharmacy bill was paid in full with a hundred dollar credit.

Smiling, Roni turned on her computer. The Christmas spirit was alive and well in Nativity.

Why had she ever doubted?

12

When Jake's Acura topped the hill overlooking Nativity around dark on Christmas Eve, the sight below caught him by surprise. The town sparkled with Christmas lights—lights that weren't there two days ago. Nativity had found their Christmas.

Grandma had died sixteen hours earlier. She had drawn her last breath quietly and with dignity, following the pattern of her entire life. He sensed there should be a lesson for him in her years of holiday grief. While he'd been a child concerned only with childish things, she'd been an adult wrestling with life's disenchantments. Now he was the adult, struggling with daily life.

He and Grandma had spent a day and a half talking. He knew her and Nativity better now than if he'd spent his entire life growing up in the town. He'd never forget her last words. "I trust you to find the meaning of my Christmas gift to you this year, Jake. It's the best present I've ever given."

While her words made no sense at the time, he assumed that he would find a wrapped gift awaiting him when he fed Max later.

He slowed for a group of carolers crossing the street in front of the administration office, rolling down his windows for a breath of fresh air. His gaze strayed to the gazebo where Christmas carols blared. Delectable smells of hot chocolate and spiced cider filled the cheerful air. A new, freshly cut cedar stood on the sidewalk, decorated with strings of popcorn and cranberries. Mismatched ornaments — representatives of the lives of Nativity's families — overflowed the tree. There was no theme or organized decorating scheme. Instead it held sentimental bauble from what he'd guess was almost every family in town. A group stood beside it, each pointing at their own contribution and sharing the story behind their trinket.

Because of the large crowd, Jake was forced to park at the rear of the building. As he climbed from the car, he heard Dusty Bitterman's voice. "This one was my boy's. I bought it for him the year he turned two." Nadine, from the post office, followed. "My granddaughter made me this one when she was in the first grade."

Instead of switching on lights, Jake followed the faint night-light burning in the mayor's office. Dropping into his office chair, he leaned back and closed his eyes.

The emotional day had taken its toll. Grandma had everything in order. She would be cremated, and buried in Springfield at Eastlawn Cemetery, next to Grandpa. She requested a short memorial service to be held in her church, and a family-only interment. The day after Christmas he would fulfill her wish. Everything would be taken care of; all Jake had to do now was face life without Grandma's wisdom and emotional support.

Tipping his head back in the chair, he focused on the Nativity replica. Tiny pieces that represented so many lives — lives whose future he'd been entrusted with.

He felt empty. Like a rudderless ship going through life.

Outside the window, Christmas carols and laughter filled the night. Judy and her husband were strolling hand in hand through the maze of lighting, their faces lit with love. And then the thought hit him. Grandma's final words made sense. *This* was the gift she'd given him this year. This town, this unquenchable spirit. Nativity with all its blemishes and blessings; the town Grandma knew and loved.

Roni. His eyes searched the gazebo area, but he failed to locate her.

His gaze shifted back to the town model in front of him. Grandma's Christmas wish. The last gift that he could give her. The last, and like hers, the best. It lay in the model. All he had to do was search for it.

For over an hour he sat in the darkness, staring at the miniature town. Once or twice he moved a piece. On the third attempt, the scene suddenly clicked. Breaking into a grin, he picked up the city limits sign and reached for a piece of paper, then scribbled something.

Taping the sign over the original city limit marker, he eased a long line of tour buses poised to enter the town. "Checkmate," Jake said to himself.

Breezing into the hardware store, Roni couldn't believe what she was about to do. Aaron glanced up, a smug grin crossing his boyish features. "Let me guess."

"That's hardly fair," she accused. "Especially with my DNA smeared all over the front window."

Walking around the counter, the clerk said. "I have one boxed and set aside with your name on it."

Roni gasped. "How could you know I'd buy that lamp? A hundred and ninety-nine dollars is a rip-off."

"Because it's Christmas, and everyone overspends at Christmas."

She handed him the money and then walked out of the hardware store, lamp in hand.

She'd done it. It was extravagant, silly, and utterly nonsensical. Anyone who hadn't seen the movie wouldn't understand the significance of the leg lamp, but Roni did. And foolish or not, that lamp now sat in her parlor window. Of course, Mary's hurricane lamp would have been more apropos, but Christmas was born of the heart, and her heart swelled with cheerfulness when she gazed at the purchase. She'd have to scrimp for the next few weeks to make up the financial expenditure, and even though she most likely wouldn't have a job by spring, she did not regret her decision. Change and risk were all that life guaranteed, and even that was fleeting. "I did it and I'm glad," she said aloud as she stepped back to adjust the taupe shade. Supple light spilled from beneath it.

Jake. She missed him dreadfully. The office had been so quiet. She had tried to reach him all day, but he wasn't answering his phone. Once, she'd called Mary's room at St. John's but there was no answer. Roni figured she was asleep and the nurse or Jake had stepped out, so she only let it ring a couple of times.

She started when she heard a knock on the window. Bending closer, she peered out and saw Jake, hands stuffed in his coat pockets, staring through the pane.

She waved.

He waved back.

"What are you doing here?" she mouthed.

"Freezing. Open the door," he mouthed back.

"Oh!" She turned and hurried to the front door and let him into the house. Shrugging out of his coat, he rubbed warmth back into his hands. "I see you finally bought that lamp."

Color crept to her cheeks. "Yes. I know it's a foolish purchase ... I didn't know that you knew I was admiring it."

"Are you kidding? You looked like a little puppy wishing for a bone every time we walked past the hardware store."

"Oh, yeah. I suppose I was pretty obvious. It's foolish, isn't it?"

He caught her hands, his eyes lit with emotion. "No, it isn't foolish. If it makes you happy, then what's foolish about it?"

"For one thing, the price. Another, some people have never seen *A Christmas Story* so they won't identify with the lamp's significance."

His gaze locked with hers. "But you do."

"Of course. And when I have children and grandchildren, we'll watch *A Christmas Story* together and the lamp will be as meaningful to them as it is to me."

He sobered, his hand tightening in hers. "Grandma passed early this morning."

"Oh ... Jake, I'm so sorry." And she had been babbling about a silly lamp. "I tried to reach you several times today."

"She went quietly. That was her way."

"Why did you come back here?"

"Because I need you."

He needed her. Roni's heart melted. Gathering him into her arms, she held him. They stood for many long moments locked in the embrace until he gently pulled back. "I have something I want to show you."

"Okay, but first I have something to show you." She reached for her coat and slipped it on.

"If you're talking about the town decorations, I've seen them."

She paused. "Are you angry?"

Shaking his head, he smiled. "I'm not angry. If I had done a better job, the town's spirit would have never been broken."

"You did your job well. You challenged the town to see what we could do without funds. You helped us discover just how important this season is to our little town. It's not about what we do, but that we do *something* to celebrate Jesus' birth.

He ruffled her hair, and then opened the door. "Let's go see my surprise."

She trailed him out of the door. Hand in hand they walked by the gazebo. Nativity was a twinkling wonderland. Their gazes traced the laughter coming from the packed gazebo where breathless skaters flew by.

"Are they *roller* skating?" he asked. About that time, Judy went down in a squeal and her husband stumbled and then piled on top of her. Sprawled on the gazebo floor, the couple's infectious laughter floated over the hillsides.

"I might have to rethink that ice rink," Jake admitted.

"Why? Roller skating is a lost art. The folks are having a great time, though I'm afraid Dusty might have cracked something. He took a hard fall earlier, but he vowed he was still intact. We can't get him to go to the hospital and have things checked out. He says to wait until he goes down a second time." They walked on. This was how life should be. She and Jake, hand in hand, walking through life with all its up and downs, together.

Her heart suddenly accelerated. What would Jake do now that his grandmother was gone? Rejoin the air force? Follow his true dream to fly? Suddenly the night didn't seem as mystical, the lights not so bright.

They reached the office, and Jake had the key in his hand.

"The office?"

"I want to show you something."

Unlocking the door, Jake ushered her inside. Switching on lights, he led the way to his desk. Roni paused. "What's going on?"

"Grandma's—and your Christmas gift." He pointed to the miniature town he'd built. Everything was in place. Every tour bus and Christmas-related shop. "This, my lady, is Nativity, Missouri. 'The Little Town That Celebrates Christmas All Year Round.'"

Roni's hand shot up to cover her mouth as she studied the board. Suddenly everything made sense. Jake's fascination with the game, the endless hours he'd spent moving pieces around. New shops, outside cafés, and stores brimming with bulbs, lights, tinsel, and Christmas paraphernalia. Switching off the overhead light, he drew her close as they studied the board. Lights twinkled from three decorated shrubs around the gazebo area. There was an ice-skating rink, along with hot chocolate and spiced cider vendors with attendants dressed as elves. There were fudge, caramel corn, and funnel cake shops galore.

"I used to dread coming to this town," he whispered against her ear. "I thought I had everything I needed or wanted. It took Grandma's gift this year to show me what was missing in my life."

"Oh Jake. I'm speechless." The gift was astonishing. He'd given Roni back her home, her children's future. "I don't know why the town hadn't thought of this earlier."

He chuckled. "With the Branson tour buses coming through almost year around, we should be able to sail through, even if things do slow down during the off-season." He flipped the overhead lights on, and moved to the board. "See, there's plenty of room to enlarge, maybe add a few children's rides, like a Candy Cane Express and Snow Cone Mountain. In time we can build new buildings and include a live nativity scene and a Christmas pageant. Jolsen's fruitcakes and rye bread will be a huge draw, and The Dairy Dream can eventually remodel and become a genuine old-fashioned ice-cream and soda parlor. We'll add fudge shops that sell peanut brittle and taffy, and Nadine will have to hire extra help at the post office to stamp 'Nativity' on all the Christmas cards that will be mailed from here each year. God willing, there are numerous ways to grow. We can put Nativity on the map." He touched her cheek. "Tradition will live on in our children."

"We'll fill Mom's old house to the rafters," she murmured then glanced up. "Children? We? Isn't this all rather sudden. You and me ... marriage."

"How long does it take to fall in love?"

She shrugged her shoulders. "I don't think there's a 'normal' time frame."

"It took less than a week for me to know how I felt about you."

She frowned. "It took you a *week*?"

He quirked a brow. "How long did it take you?"

"Truthfully?" She grinned. "About the same time."

Overwhelmed, Roni stepped back into his arms. He had given her the greatest Christmas present ever. Love, tradition, and a home. It made the set of sockets she'd purchased for him at Steil's look puny. At the moment she felt like she would follow him to the ends of the earth, but Nativity was home. Springfield was nice, but this town was her life. Could she leave? Even for this wonderful man? "Jake. I know this is all so new to both of us, but I love it here. Where will we call home?"

Smiling, he met her expectant gaze. "That's up to you and the town. I'd like to run the transformation, but folks here might feel differently. I'm not exactly their favorite person."

"Nonsense. Most understand what you've done, and the ones who don't will answer to me. You saved the town."

"It's not saved yet," he corrected. "The town will still have to sacrifice; in order for the plan to work everyone has to pull together. There's still much to be done."

Their lips touched, then lingered. Finally she whispered. "I love you, Jake Brisco."

"The feeling is mutual, Roni Elliot. Merry Christmas."

"Merry Christmas, darling."

Offering his arm, he said, "Hey. Before we attend Christmas Eve services, could we get a cup of that hot chocolate with that candy cane that you're always harping about?"

"Harping!" She playfully boxed his shoulder. "Just for that remark we don't have time, but we will later. And we'll skate." She paused and looked at him. "How did you know we have hot chocolate this year?"

"Because there's not much about you that I don't know, Roni Elliott. Dusty Bitterman's told me your whole life's story over recent lunches. He thought the information might come in handy since—and these are his words—'Eventually I'm not going to be able to live without you'."

"And to know me is to love me," she agreed.

He winked. "I'm still adjusting to the idea."

Tucking her arm through his, Jake proceeded to the church where the ringing bell beckoned worshipers. As Roni climbed the stairs ahead of him, he paused and turned to look up. Overhead, flickering starlight formed a frosty canopy.

Thanks, he said softly. *I owe you one.*

AUTHOR'S NOTE

Copeland Christmases are loud and fun. Every year God blesses our lives with growth: new babies, new girlfriends, and new wives. The immediate family now totals sixteen and growing. Audrey was the lone granddaughter until December 7, 2008, when Anabelle joined the crowd.

We begin our Christmas Eve celebration with a church service, then head home to eat enchiladas. I know, enchiladas aren't exactly a festive dish, but it's my family's most requested holiday meal. I'm not a big decorator anymore, but we have a tree and presents. The smallest children get to play "Santa." They deliver the mound of packages to each recipient seated in a circle. We agree to open one gift at time, when it's our turn, so everyone can see and enjoy the surprise, but after the second or third present chaos breaks out and all semblance of order is gone.

As I wrote *The Christmas Lamp*, I realized that tradition is priceless, whether you have a small family, a large family, or no family. I don't have any one particular custom other than the tree, presents, and our Christmas Eve church service. This particular sacred hour draws our family into an indelible bond, one we remember all year long, though we may not see each other for weeks at a time. We attend different churches, different denominations, but on Christmas Eve we are one.

As God always does, he gives me an idea and weeks later I see the evidence of his hand in the project.

We live thirty miles from Branson, Missouri, and we visit the town and the Landing often. There's a five and ten in the 'old downtown' district. One day we parked in front of the five and ten store, and there it was. The lamp. The gaudy, fishnet stocking leg featured in my favorite holiday classic film, *A Christmas Story.*

I had to have that lamp.

It happened to be my birthday, and my husband had asked for the third or fourth time what I wanted? When I saw the lamp I said, "That lamp." He laughed and we walked on through the store. At least twice more, I said I wanted the lamp, and every time he would laugh or say, "You can't be serious." But I was serious. When I left the store without the lamp I was hopping mad. How dare he ask what I wanted for my birthday, and then laugh when I told him? I suppose it finally sank in that I actually wanted the lamp when I wouldn't speak to him on the way home. Forgive me, Lord.

The next morning, he announced that we were going back to Branson to get the lamp. With a sincere hug, he apologized and asked for forgiveness; he really *didn't* believe that I would want that lamp in our home. To him, the lamp was a garish gadget with no significance. To me, it represented family struggles, raising children, man and woman accepting each other's faults and loving each other anyway—the true heart of Christmas, and Christ's love in admittedly, a different form.

We purchased the lamp, and last Thanksgiving night we ceremoniously placed the lamp in the window, where it will sit each Christmas season. The children had a wonderful time assembling the lamp, and I even heard some giggles and laughs from the adults.

I pray they will see it as a joyful tradition they will carry on with their children and grandchildren. Maybe they'll even argue over it like fine china. Tradition doesn't have to be logical; it only has to emphasize the light of Christ and his everlasting love. When I turn on the leg lamp, I'll remember the one who has given me a sense of humor, and a heart filled with gratitude for the light that he has brought into my life.

May God richly bless you and his light shine in your life all year through.

Merry Christmas,
Lori Copeland

Unwrapping Christmas

Lori Copeland

It's that time of year again, and with excitement and high expectations, Rose has planned the perfect Christmas for her family and friends. But when she feels them drifting away during a time that should celebrate togetherness, Rose is forced to slow down in the most unexpected way. In this whimsical, uplifting story, she discovers the true meaning of giving.

Hardcover, Jacketed: 978-0-310-27226-7

Pick up a copy today at your favorite bookstore!

Now and Always

Lori Copeland

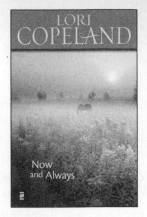

Very few things distract Katie Addison when she's on a mission, whether it's opening her home to abused women, rehabilitating injured horses, or helping tall, gorgeous Warren Tate mend his broken heart. But when financial difficulties pile up for her, Katie hesitantly admits she herself may need help.

Since his fiance left him, Warren is done with women—especially independent women, which he'd guess describes Katie Addison to a tee. Reluctantly he agrees to help Katie with her financial troubles. But when his budget doesn't include Katie's daily lattes, Warren realizes he may have a challenging client on his hands.

Meanwhile, Sheriff Ben O'Keefe can't seem to get Katie's attention. Everyone in town knows he has had a longstanding crush on her. But to Katie, Ben is just Ben. When mysterious events turn Katie to him for help, is it the chance Ben has been waiting for?

Softcover: 978-0-310-26351-7

Pick up a copy today at your favorite bookstore!

Simple Gifts

Lori Copeland

Can anything else go wrong? Marlene Queens goes home to Parnass Springs, Missouri, to put her late Aunt Beth's house on the market and settle the estate. But once she's back home, Marlene suddenly finds herself in over her head. Her Aunt Ingrid grows more demanding by the day. Marlene discovers her childhood sweetheart is now the local vet and the town's acting mayor. And when a group of citizens want to put up a statue in memory of Marlene's father — the parent who always embarrassed her as a child — Marlene is unwillingly swept into a firestorm of controversy.

As one thing leads to another, Marlene sees her entire life being rearranged before her eyes. Parnass Springs may never be the same. Marlene fears that the secret she's kept for years may be revealed. Can God work a miracle so she can finally have the future she's longed for?

Softcover: 978-0-310-26350-0

Pick up a copy today at your favorite bookstore!

Monday Morning Faith

Lori Copeland

Dear Mom and Pop,

Two days ago we all spent the afternoon in palm trees. One of the village dogs broke his leash and treed the whole community. The dog is mean, but I have managed to form a cautious relationship with him by feeding him scraps from our table, and jelly beans ... I hope candy doesn't hurt a dog; it hasn't hurt this dog, I can assure you.

I know you're wondering about Sam ... I love him with all my heart, but sometimes love isn't enough.

Love always,
Johanna

Librarian Johanna Holland likes her simple life in Saginaw, Michigan. So why is she standing in the middle of the New Guinea Jungle? Johanna is simply aghast at the lack of hot showers and ... well ... clothing! She is positive the mission field is most certainly not God's plan for her life, but will that mean letting go of the man she loves? Warm and whimsical, *Monday Morning Faith* will take you on a spiritual journey filled with depth and humor.

Softcover: 978-0-310-26349-4

Pick up a copy today at your favorite bookstore!

Share Your Thoughts

With the Author: Your comments will be forwarded to the author when you send them to *zauthor@zondervan.com*.

With Zondervan: Submit your review of this book by writing to *zreview@zondervan.com*.

Free Online Resources at
www.zondervan.com

Zondervan AuthorTracker: Be notified whenever your favorite authors publish new books, go on tour, or post an update about what's happening in their lives.

Daily Bible Verses and Devotions: Enrich your life with daily Bible verses or devotions that help you start every morning focused on God.

Free Email Publications: Sign up for newsletters on fiction, Christian living, church ministry, parenting, and more.

Zondervan Bible Search: Find and compare Bible passages in a variety of translations at www.zondervanbiblesearch.com.

Other Benefits: Register yourself to receive online benefits like coupons and special offers, or to participate in research.